THE DAWN PALACE

Other Books by H. M. Hoover

Children of Morrow
The Delikon
Return to Earth
The Lost Star
This Time of Darkness
Another Heaven, Another Earth
The Bell Tree
The Shepherd Moon
Orvis

THE DAWN PALACE

The Story of Medea

BY H. M. HOOVER

E. P. DUTTON   NEW YORK

Special thanks to Ray Ceriotti, B.S., ChE; M.B.A., for his help in researching the uses made of raw crude oil and naphtha, circa 1500–1000 B.C.

Library of Congress Cataloging-in-Publication Data

Hoover, H. M.
   The Dawn Palace.

   Summary: Having been trained in supernatural knowledge, thirteen-year-old Medea finds herself in a unique position to help when the Greek hero Jason comes to her father's kingdom in search of the Golden Fleece.
      1. Medea (Greek mythology)—Juvenile fiction.
   2. Jason (Greek mythology)—Juvenile fiction.
   [1. Medea (Greek mythology)—Fiction.   2. Jason (Greek mythology)—Fiction]   I. Title.
   PZ7.H7705Daw   1988   [Fic]   87–30602
   ISBN 0–525–44388–6

Published in the United States by E. P. Dutton, 2 Park Avenue, New York, N.Y. 10016, a division of NAL Penguin Inc.

Published simultaneously in Canada by Fitzhenry & Whiteside Limited, Toronto

Editor: Ann Durell   Designer: Riki Levinson

Printed in the U.S.A.   W   First Edition
10 9 8 7 6 5 4 3 2 1

to Rosie
with love and gratitude

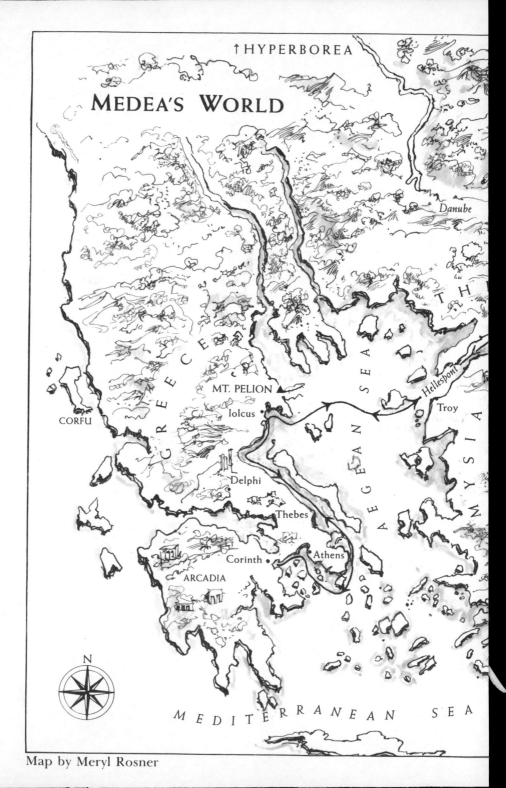

MEDEA'S WORLD

↑HYPERBOREA

Danube

TH

GREECE

MT. PELION ▲

Iolcus

Hellespont

Troy

CORFU

AEGEAN SEA

MYSIA

Delphi

Thebes

Corinth • Athens

ARCADIA

N

M E D I T E R R A N E A N   S E A

Map by Meryl Rosner

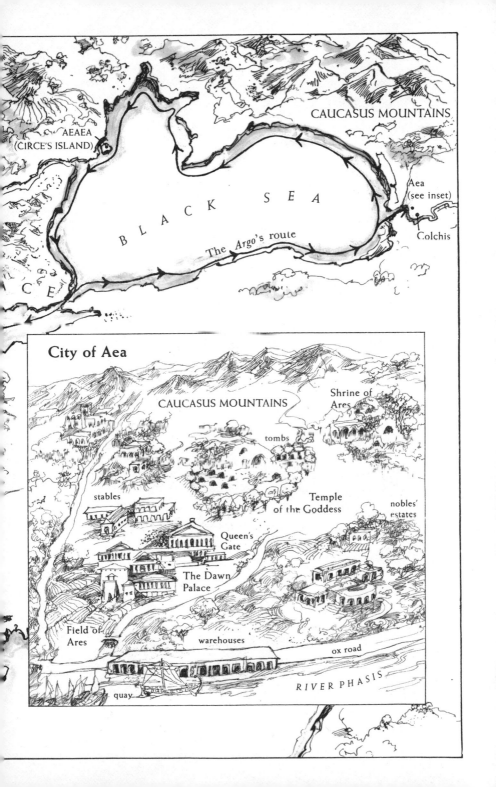

CAUCASUS MOUNTAINS

AEAEA
(CIRCE'S ISLAND)

Aea
(see inset)

Colchis

B L A C K   S E A

The *Argo*'s route

C E

C

E

City of Aea

CAUCASUS MOUNTAINS

Shrine of
Ares

tombs

stables

Temple
of the Goddess

nobles'
estates

Queen's
Gate

The Dawn
Palace

Field of
Ares

warehouses

ox road

quay

RIVER PHASIS

PART ONE

ONE

IN THE DAWN PALACE lived a family not entirely human. Their youngest child was named Medea.

She was five years old the night she was wakened by a silence so complete that she held her breath to listen. All she could see was an oblong of moonlight framing three of the white horses painted on the wall. The horses looked frozen in a swift and silent race, nostrils flaring, manes and tails blowing in an unseen wind. Outside no dogs barked, no nightingales or frogs or insects sang. There wasn't a sound within the palace, not so much as a snore. When she finally dared to move, her covers whispered against her body, and she breathed a sigh of relief to know she hadn't gone deaf in her sleep.

Pushing aside the curtain, she peered into the gloom. Her slave, Lukka, was a soft, dark shape on her pallet by the door. A dog lay beside her, its muzzle cradled on the woman's feet. Reassured by the familiar, the child slid off her couch. The stone floor was cold.

To reach the window, she stepped from fleece to fleece, as if crossing a ford.

In the courtyard everything looked normal. The moon was full and bright, the sky star-filled. Between the shadows of the cypress, wavelets glimmered on the reservoir. The fountains had been turned off. She leaned her elbows on the cold sill and took a deep breath. The air smelled of pine and river and wood-smoke.

Movement caught her eye. A cat was crossing the gravel, tail high, tip waving. For no reason the animal stopped and then sat down, creating a long, dark shadow. It seemed to be watching something across the way.

As she glanced in that direction, a man came out of the arch to the second courtyard, crossed over to the Queen's Gate, opened it and went out. A second man followed and then three women. All were strangers, oddly dressed, each carrying a blanket roll. They made no noise. Thieves? Medea was about to call Lukka and the guards when a tall woman came out into the moon-lit courtyard. There was no mistaking who it was—her mother, Asterodeia, the queen.

She wore a white cloak that swept the ground, and moonlight glittered off diamond crystals fastened in her long black hair. Halfway across the yard she turned and looked back, then raised her hand in farewell, as if she could see her daughter watching. Medea shivered and stepped back into the shadows, afraid without knowing why. She saw the cat run to the queen, who knelt and picked it up. With her chin pressed against the animal's head, Asterodeia followed the strangers. The gate closed behind her, seemingly of its own volition.

More curious now than frightened, the child ran back to her couch and, picking up one of the covers as a shawl, hurried from the room. She stepped carefully over Lukka and the dog, tiptoed around the screen into the outer room, and ran through the hall beyond. Servants slept on the risers of the corner hearth. The burning logs glowed dull red beneath a coat of white ash. No one stirred as Medea passed.

Just beyond the apartment of Chalciope, her widowed sister, in the center of the women's wing, was an open hall and stairwell leading to the roof. The worn steps were high for her short legs. Twice she scuffed her knees against the rough stone. Gaining the roof, she heard a horse whinny at the Queen's Gate. She ran, but by the time she reached a vantage point, there was nothing to see, not even hoofprints.

The gravel in front of the gate was unshadowed, as if it had been freshly raked. Puzzled, she looked beyond the citadel to where the moon made a broad white path across the swollen river. There in the distance ran the queen's white mare with the other horses following. Now distinct, now hidden by trees, they moved along the winding road. At the base of the hill where the road forked, they turned east toward the Caucasus. She watched them until a cloud drifted across the moon and they were lost in darkness.

She stood there waiting, wondering if they were going to come back. They didn't. After a while a toad trilled softly, and tree frogs remembered to sing. A wolf howled in the hills across the river; another answered from the hill behind the palace. Down at the stables the watchdogs began to bark, and trees rustled in a breeze. She shivered and climbed down from the wall.

By the time she reached her room and bed, the night was back to normal. She fell asleep wondering where the queen had gone at such an odd hour.

It was daylight and raining when Lukka woke her. "Hurry and dress. Your father wants you in the Hall."

"It's cold," Medea complained, groggy, wondering why Lukka sounded upset.

"Yes. Wear this." Lukka pulled a soft white chamois gown from the bedside chest. "And this." She laid a gold tiara atop the gown, a bib-shaped neckpiece and gold bracelets. "Hurry!"

A woman of nineteen, Lukka had been brought to Colchis as a child, a captive from a raid on some barbaric northern tribe. She had red hair, dark blue eyes and skin that freckled easily in this southern sun. Because of her exotic looks, she had been trained as a bed slave but proved too temperamental. She was a biter, it was said, and she bit from outrage, not passion.

Too rare to sell and too beautiful to mar by brand or whip, she had been demoted to bath slave. Toas, the chief chamberlain, the eunuch who managed the royal household, decided she should be used for breeding. If she was not tractable, perhaps her offspring would be. And so it happened that when Lukka was nursing her first son, she was assigned as wet nurse to the infant princess. When Medea was weaned, the slave was sent back to her bath duties, but Medea had raged and sobbed so inconsolably that Toas was forced to relent. Lukka was given to Medea, to the great satisfaction of both.

"Have royal visitors come?" Medea asked now as she came up the steps from her bathroom. Guests might explain the queen's curious ride in the night—perhaps she'd ridden out to meet someone?

"All the nobles have come." Lukka pulled the linen shift up over the girl's curly black hair.

"Why?"

"Your father will explain."

The princess frowned; she did not like mysteries. "Tell me now," she said, and when Lukka didn't, added as inducement, "I'll whip you if you don't."

"When you're dressed I'll go find the whip for you," said Lukka. "Now raise your arms." The soft leather enveloped the girl; the gown smelled of cedar chips.

Irked, the child imagined whipping her servant, inflicting pain, perhaps cutting that soft back. As her head emerged into daylight, she winced and impulsively reached up to touch the woman's face in apology for her threat.

Lukka had no time for tenderness. "Turn around," she said.

"I saw the queen ride out last night," Medea said as the tight-fitting gown was smoothed down, "with five strangers." Lukka's hands paused. "She took the gray cat with her."

The young woman made a visible effort to conceal her thoughts as she tied the blue drawstring at the waist of the dress. "You were dreaming."

"No!" As proof, the child elaborated.

"You climbed the steps in the dark? Alone?" Lukka interrupted at that point. "If you'd fallen, you could have been badly hurt, and I would have been whipped! I'm responsible for you."

"But I didn't fall. . . . Why are those women chanting?"

[7]

Above the hiss of rain on the courtyard gravel the eerie ululations of priestesses had begun to echo from somewhere inside the palace. Suddenly a woman screamed, as if in terror and pain. By the time the arch of sound ended in mid-breath, the ululations had become twice as loud to cover the noise. Both woman and child went still at the scream. Now their glances met, the child's troubled, the woman's wide with the fear only a vulnerable slave could understand.

Recovering herself, Lukka reached for the girl's sandals. "Hurry. The escort is waiting in the anteroom."

"I don't want to go. Something bad is happening."

"You have no choice."

"You come with me." The command was plaintive.

"I can't. You know that."

Because of the rain, Medea was escorted through the palace. There were no halls. Rooms opened into rooms, each larger and higher than the last. Unless she looked up, which was beneath her dignity, her view of the two men flanking her consisted of glimpses of bare brown knees flashing in and out between the pleats of their brown leather skirts. The men smelled of sweet oil, leather, and brass. Their sandals scuffed over the stone floor, and their shields and swords whispered *rish-rush* against their thighs as they walked.

The priestesses were chanting in the queen's private courtyard. Medea caught a glimpse of them through an arcade. All were painted in mourning, dull reds, yellow ochers, and black. They looked frightening, inhuman.

The Hall of Audience was two stories high, the roof supported by double rows of sandstone pillars painted red. Torches flared along the walls. Oil lamps hung from the rafters. The room smelled of smoke, damp stone, wet wool, and too many bodies in one place. Not only all of the nobles and their wives but all of the royal chamberlains and staff were gathered there. Loud ritual wails enveloped her as the doors were opened. Faces turned in her direction, and a ragged, makeshift aisle formed.

At the far end of the aisle, seated on the elevated platform in the queen's customary place was Chalciope, wearing a tragic expression. She was dressed in white, the color of mourning. Her face was also painted for mourning, and her blonde hair hung lank from the rain. Behind her stood her four sons, blond also and as graduated as stairsteps in height. Beside her sat King Aeetes, his jowls quivering with grief. Seeing her father cry, Medea forgot her dignity. She ran to him and climbed upon his lap before anyone could stop her.

King Aeetes had one withered ear, the left, which was purplish brown and shiny and curled tightly against his head like a rotted leaf. He tried to keep it covered beneath his fringe of white hair. His mouth was pink and pursed, his eyes small, pale-lashed and shrewd as a pig's. Those loyal to him said that he was round as the sun, but others, less kind, whispered that he looked more like an onion with legs. For comfort he wore a loose linen gown belted by a rope of gold mesh. Sandals with four-inch-thick soles compensated for his shortness. His partial baldness was hidden by his crown, an elaborate garland of oak leaves and acorns. Any movement made the acorns shiver on their stems and chime against each other like tiny golden bells. He

[9]

wore his crown at a jaunty angle with the rim resting against that left ear. In time the weight of the gold, cushioned though it was by a felt undercap, had cut off circulation, causing the ear to wither.

The acorns jangled gaily as Aeetes' small daughter put her arms around his neck. "Why are you crying, Father?" She pressed her smooth cheek against his wet, grizzled one. "Why is everyone in mourning?"

"For the same reason even the sky weeps. Queen Asterodeia is dead." Aeetes' weight caused him to wheeze slightly when he spoke.

Medea leaned away from him and stared into his pale blue eyes, shocked. "Did her mare throw her?"

He frowned. "She died on her couch. Her women found her."

"After she returned from her ride?"

"She wasn't riding." The king's grief was tinged with impatience as he wiped tears from the crease in his chin.

"But she went riding. I saw her. In the moonlight. At first I thought the strangers were thieves, but then she came out and went with them. . . ." She told him what she'd seen from her window. His gaze never left her face, and his right arm, embracing her, stiffened.

Those standing closest to the dais pressed forward to hear, some of them making gestures for silence. The wailing died away. Chalciope, after listening for a moment, whispered to a servant, who hurried from the room.

"You are an infant," Aeetes said when she had finished, "but try to understand. Think. If what you've said had truly happened, the queen's guards would have known—as would her maids. The grooms would have been roused to ready her mare. The dogs would have barked. And I would have known."

As he spoke there was a little commotion at the back of the room, and Medea twisted about to see. The high priestess from the Temple of the Goddess was being ushered into the room. The old woman's face was tear-ravaged, her withered breasts blood-flecked and welted with self-inflicted nail scratches to show how much she grieved. Chalciope rose to speak with the old woman in urgent, worried whispers.

"She says you were granted a vision," Chalciope whispered to her little sister as she returned to her seat. "She says also that you are not to speak about it again. You may provoke unnecessary speculation. You are the last and the only virgin daughter of Asterodeia, and someday you will be a temple priestess. As such, what you say now can be—uh—misinterpreted." Chalciope then turned to the audience. "The princess was troubled by dreams. The high priestess assures me that we may discount the visions of one still so close to infancy."

There were sympathetic murmurs from some, speculative silence from others.

Still seated on the king's knee, Medea studied her sister's face. Kohl lined Chalciope's eyelids and made her brows one continuous black slash across her forehead. Below the kohl, blue powder arched over each eye. Below the blue was chalk white. On each cheek was a large dot of red ochre, and over all this more red and umber had been smeared. She looked again at her father. His face—like Chalciope's—was suitably sad but otherwise unreadable. He wore no mourning colors. But if the queen was dead . . . ? She slid to the floor, saying, "I want to see the queen now."

"No!" Chalciope stood up in agitation. "Not yet. She's not—"

"Yes." Aeetes' crown chimed as he took a deep breath and heaved himself to his feet. "The child must see her mother. We will go with her."

The body of the queen and those of four of her handmaidens lay on trestle tables in the audience chamber of the Women's Court. The room smelled damp and high with the spices used to cover the odor of blood. There was also an overlay of an unpleasant sulfurous scent. Outside the priestesses chanted. As the king and his daughters entered, three priestesses were working at a table draped with royal red cloth. On it lay the body of the queen. They were obviously surprised to see Aeetes but quickly recovered and, after a last few ministrations, scurried from the room.

Standing between sister and father, Medea looked carefully at the stillness on each table. The bodies had been bathed, rubbed with oil and ground spices, and gowned in fine Egyptian cotton gauze. The slender feet were clean, the toenails carefully painted red. The face masks were in place, the queen's of beaten gold, her women's carved red jasper. The bodies looked like recumbent statues. She felt sorry for them all.

Because it was custom, she knew without being told that the maidens had been killed so that their spirits could be set free to care for the queen on her journey back to the Mother. She guessed that one of them, dying, was responsible for the scream that had frightened her and Lukka. Perhaps none had wanted to die for their queen.

"Do you believe me now?"

Medea looked up at her father. "I can't see her face."

"It *is* the queen." Aeetes' tone said there would be no more questions.

"Come along now." Chalciope escorted her back to her rooms. "You must not repeat your story," she told her as they walked. "You will only upset people, and there is no time for that. There's too much to be done. Beacons must be oiled and fired in this rain to send the news to the towns up and down the river. We must send messengers to the hill villages, the mines, the distant villas along the coast. The funeral feast must be prepared. It will last nine days. Guests will be arriving with their retinues, horses, and slaves. All must be fed and housed. I will be busy. Toas will be busy. Even Lukka must help us with the preparations. The king and I wish you to behave with the dignity of your rank. Do you understand?"

She did. For the rest of the day she wandered about, ignored and bored. When the rain let up and no one was watching her, she left her rooms and went down to the stables, directly to the stall where the queen's favorite horse was kept. Asterodeia's white mare had a faint gray patch above its tail. Its eyes were black with long black lashes. The horse now in the stall was a true albino; its pale eyes were pink-rimmed and its coat pure of color. She hadn't been dreaming the night before— wherever the queen had gone, she had ridden away on her favorite mare.

Before sunset the following day, the biers were loaded onto five high-wheeled, red-canopied oxcarts. The great gong was struck three times and while the reverberations still echoed, the Queen's Gate swung open. Led by the chanting priestesses, the funeral procession filed out of the courtyard and wound along the muddy road across the hilltop and up, to the top of the adjoining hill.

Behind the queen's cart walked the royal family, flanked by King Aeetes' Corinthian guard, who walked with shields nearly touching, their swords drawn in salute. Honored guests, nobles, and their families came next, followed by the handmaidens' carts. The long cortege moved at the speed of the oxen, to the sound of ritual wailing and throbbing drums. The rain continued to fall; the river ran yellow with mud.

Dressed in finery and jewels, kept dry by a hooded sharkskin cape and boots, the Princess Medea appeared indifferent to the somber drama. Instead of weeping, she watched birds flee the noise, admired the wild crocus and violets in the grass, paid attention to leaves quivering under the impact of raindrops, and thus caused people to remark on her lack of feeling, especially when compared to Chalciope, who wailed with proper fervor.

The last few hundred yards of road were steep; rain had turned the track to slippery mud. The oxen slipped, bellowed, and rolled their eyes in confusion. The crack of whips punctuated the chanting and the drums.

The trees at the summit were old. Where one of the giants had fallen and sunlight could penetrate the canopy, azalea, dogwood and crab apple blossoms made dense mists of color in the rain. Paths between the pillarlike trunks led to beehive-shaped tombs. Here a dozen different queens slept. Other, older tombs were cut cavelike into the hillside.

The road led between great jumbles of stone whose roughness, half hidden by ferny moss and vines, held sun-rotted crystals that gleamed like jelly in the wet. Before remembered time, a portion of the hill had weathered away, exposing these slabs of granite and a large, dome-ceilinged cavern, the outermost chamber of a huge cave. In time a new outer wall was built and the chamber made into a temple. The matriarchy found the place ideal for the mysteries of their religion.

The oxcarts halted in a line at the bottom of the steps. Silence fell. As the mud-flecked retinue gathered around the carts or took shelter under the clifflike overhang beside the temple entrance, the two princesses climbed the steps alone.

King Aeetes helped to lift his queen's bier from the cart and give it into the care of the priestesses. Seemingly laden as much by grief as with his own bulk, he followed them and their burden up the shallow steps. Because men were forbidden to enter the temple, he stopped beneath the stone lintel of the entrance and waited, weeping with silent dignity, until all the biers were carried past him into the darkness. When the last of the women had entered the temple, he turned and slowly walked down the steps and hoisted himself onto an oxcart to be driven back to the Dawn Palace. He would never see Asterodeia again.

Medea had been in the temple once before. She remembered that visit now only because of the smells— a mixture of damp stone, lichen, and stale incense. Before going deeper into the gloom, she stopped and turned for one last look at daylight, the bright glow of sunset behind the clouds. Her sister impatiently clutched her arm so hard that fingernails dug in.

"Everyone is watching! Remember who you are!"

"I know who I am."

"Then act like it! Don't make me ashamed."

Inside the high-domed cavern, lamps burned behind thin curtains of flowstone. They created glowing points of muted earth colors. Along the walls the torches flared and hissed in mysterious drafts. Stalactites glistened on the ceiling. Behind the altar, where lamps always burned, velvety red lichen covered the wall. Moss grew below each torch bracket. Where the rear wall of the cavern failed to meet the floor, there was a reflecting pool that mirrored half the chamber.

Medea walked with her hands clasped behind her back, her head uptilted to better admire the beauty of the place.

"Walk properly!" hissed her sister.

A servant emerged from the gloom to take their rain gear. Another brought white woolen wraps to keep their shoulders warm.

In the center of the chamber was a depression some thirty feet across, paved with a cobblestone of human skulls. From that pavement rose, almost to the ceiling, the statue of the Goddess. Carved from an enormous white stalagmite, in situ, she stood on a three-tiered pedestal, each tier ringed with flickering lamps. In contrast to the macabre pavement, her expression—and especially her smile—was one of great gentleness. Everything about her was round, all lines soft, all edges blurred. Her nose was little more than a daub; her neck was short, her hair pulled back and bound by a thong to reveal small, close-fitting ears. Her eyelids were lowered as if she slept or gazed down beneath long lashes. She wore what appeared to be a long-sleeved tunic and loose trousers tied at the ankles. The sculptor had made her feet endearingly small, her hands and fingers long and elegantly tapered. Her left hand was cupped against her waist, the right raised in greeting or benediction.

Medea stood beside her sister and watched as the priestesses, moving in ritual cadence, carried in the biers. Those of the handmaidens were put on the two lower tiers of the statue's pedestal. With some effort but no loss of dignity, the priestesses lifted the queen's bier to the top tier, to rest directly beneath the Goddess's gaze. More torches were lit. Jars of burning incense were placed between the pallets. Musk pods were broken.

The head priestess prostrated herself in supplication, arms outflung, sinewy hands beating a rhythmic grief. The death ceremony began. "You who are starlight and gift from the stars, beloved of mortals, nymph of the mountains, rejoice! Rejoice!" the priestesses chanted and the caverns echoed. "You return to all that you are, are again what you once were."

The chanting became progressively more emotional, more dramatic, and the women of the royal household were duty bound to listen. It was seldom that the priestesses had the chance to display their entire repertoire before such a distinguished audience. They took full advantage of the situation.

While the ceremony went on, in the side galleries tables were being set up and food and wine put out, as well as sleeping pallets so that some mourners might rest while others kept vigil through the long night.

Her own innate sense of dignity kept the five-year-old standing patiently through the long ceremony—dignity and the knowledge that eventually she could sit down and rest and eat. She was tired and hungry, and the smoke burned her eyes.

Early darkness fell; rain and fog made the warm, well-lighted cave a refuge. The smoky air was redolent with the smell of food, incense, and opium. Trying to stay awake at the table, sit erect, and remain dignified after her stomach was full of rich food and wine, Medea heard the women's voices fade in and out of sense, along with the incessant chanting. The second time she swayed and jerked herself back to semiconsciousness, Lukka stepped out of the shadows and came to her side to whisper that a bed was ready if she wished to retire. The women rose in respect as she left them. Only Chalciope remained seated.

She was led to a rounded side chamber with walls scoured smooth by ancient gravel. On a tiny ledge a lamp with a copper reflector gave light enough to see the mound of bedding on the floor. Removing only her boots, Medea crawled between the fleeces, too sleepy to acknowledge Lukka's good-night caress. But when Lukka left the room, the girl's eyes flew open to make sure the lamp had been left burning.

The air here was cool and clean. She took a deep breath and had just closed her eyes when she heard the chanting approach and then slowly fade away and guessed that the priestesses were going back into that part of the cave forbidden to all but themselves. Back there, it was said, was a long passage with walls etched with sacred inscriptions, and a tunnel that led down endlessly, into the Womb of Earth. Down there, so it was said, the First Children of Earth still lived, and other things besides. When the Nine called their own secret names, there would be answering cries and whispers. Only the Nine knew why, or what was said and learned. Someday she too would be a priestess, like Chalciope, and have to go down there. Medea shivered at the thought and fell into troubled sleep.

Something touched her leg!

She sat up, instantly awake, and found Chalciope and two cousins sleeping beside her. Their breaths smelled of wine and herbs; their long hair was stale with smoke, musk, and oil. She wrinkled her nose in disgust and edged away, her child's sense of purity offended. A torch still burned in the outer passage; pale orange light and shadows wavered on the walls. A rat sidled past the door, whiskers twitching. Somewhere close by cave water was trickling, a sound so suggestive that once heard, could not be ignored. She got up and hurried outside.

The rain had stopped, but the air was heavy. Mist floated. As she ran down the steps, a large animal crashed away through the brush. She stopped, heart pounding. A distant panther caterwauled, and the forest went still. When a tree frog trilled again and the night music resumed, she allowed need to win out over fear. Cold mud squelched between her toes and a dozen mosquitoes bit her before she regained the protection of the smoky temple.

All was quiet now. Almost all the torches had guttered out; the altar and funeral lamps flickered. The Goddess stood glistening in the wavering light. In the gallery where the food was served, four priestesses slept at the table, arms serving as pillows, sacred masks beside them on the benches. Near the altar a woman lay cocooned in a bearskin, her face bathed in sweat, even though she shivered in her sleep. Another sat against a wall, naked, limp, chin on chest, snoring. The floor was littered with tiny opium-paste jars.

Absentmindedly scratching mosquito bites, Medea took this all in, disappointed to see the priestesses diminished by sleep, their mystery gone. Without their masks she knew them all—the four at the table were noblewomen; the one on the floor was the queen's cook. And if spirits walked in the night, shouldn't someone be awake to guard? Or was this carelessness because the vigil wasn't truly for the queen?

When she turned and looked up at the body wearing the golden mask, her gaze was as single-minded as a stalking lion's. Her nose wrinkled with distaste as she picked her way across the cobble of skulls and quickly climbed the first two tiers—being careful not to touch the lamps and incense burners that stood between the handmaidens. Standing on the second tier, she leaned over the cold stillness that was the queen, took a deep breath and pulled at the mask. It didn't budge. To her horror, the head and narrow shoulders moved, then lifted as she tugged. The scent of perfumed oil made her dizzy.

Carefully lowering the head, she stopped to think, then ran a forefinger around the edge of the mask. Daubs of beeswax held the gold in place. She tried to free those, one by one. The skin stretched until it threatened to tear, but the wax held. Her persistent fingers pried and tugged until suddenly the mask came free and she nearly dropped it. In her panic, her warm elbow touched a breast so cold it seemed to burn. She gasped and then quickly glanced around. None of the sleepers stirred. Breathing a sigh of relief, she looked at the face. It wasn't her mother.

With clinical curiosity, she studied the stranger's face, wondering who this was and how the young woman had come to end here. Not that it mattered; it was probably a slave, kept in hiding until needed. With a sigh, Medea replaced the mask, resolutely pushing it back down onto the wax.

"Are you satisfied?"

The voice from the shadows below frightened her so badly that she nearly fell off the pedestal. Her heart, already beating in her ears, stopped and jumped sideways before resuming at a rackety pace.

"What will you do with your knowledge, Medea?" The voice was soft but insistent, very sure of itself. And completely unfamiliar.

As a princess of Colchis, she couldn't show fear. Or turn around to see who was awake to threaten her. She steadied herself against the stone, checked to make sure the mask was on properly, and then, with great deliberation, climbed down. Reaching the safety of the floor, she dusted off her hands and straightened her gown before looking to see who dared to address her so familiarly.

On the other side of the circle of dim light and reflected by the pool stood a woman in a blue Tyrian robe and gold sandals. She was tall and beautiful, with rare wheaten hair and eyes as green as a cat's. In the hollow of her throat nestled a green gem bound in gold wire. She was smiling, as if in rueful recognition and acceptance of the inevitable.

Medea returned the steady gaze. "Who are you?"

"I am Circe."

Pride and self-control were shattered. Medea stared openmouthed, afraid. Aeetes had told her all about this sister of his; he forbade anyone to speak her name in the Dawn Palace for fear of summoning death by her wrath, and when he spoke of her, he always made signs to ward off evil. He had also said that she was terribly ugly.

Circe ruled the Isle of Dawn, Aeaea, and had no love of people. The very name of her island, Aeetes said, came from the sound of the wailing of her victims. More fortress than dwelling, her palace had massive walls of earth and stone. It had been built around a spring that emptied into a brook, which cut across the grounds and out beneath a wall. The forest around her palace was full of enormous oaks, which she allowed no one to cut. Wolves and lions roamed freely and were so tame that they would approach travelers and try to speak . . . because they were all men, enchanted, trapped there forever by Circe. At night strange lights flickered over the island, and weird sobbing echoed through the trees.

So her father told her. But seeing this beautiful woman with the gently mocking smile calmed Medea's fears. For some reason her father had not told the truth. Always afterward she would remember this thrill of sudden learning, this first glimpse of the gulf that might exist between reputation and reality.

"What will you do with your knowledge?" Circe repeated. "You worked so hard to gain it. You must have had a purpose in doing so."

Medea hadn't thought past the urge to tell, to insist that others see her truth as their own. But as she looked up into Circe's eyes, it occurred to her that other people *already knew.* Perhaps not the king, but certainly the women who had prepared the bodies, the priestesses. Especially the high priestess, who had to verify the death of any queen of the ruling house. And if the truth became known, what of the families of the queen's handmaidens? All were powerful nobles who would not be pleased to learn their daughters had died for an impostor. If others shared her secret, it was for good reason, and it wouldn't be wise to let them know what she had just learned. Being a child would offer no protection. Poison was swift and sure, especially for a princess.

"Keep it to myself?"

"A wise decision."

"But I don't understand. If she's not dead—"

"She has gone." Circe's pronouncement, in tones so resonant that the fragile pipestones thrilled, made the queen's absence permanent, final. "She has gone to her palace in the high mountains, where no mortals can go. She won't return."

"But why?"

There was a pause before Circe answered. "When men began to speak of the Dawn Palace belonging not to her but to Aeetes, she knew the worship of Earth the Mother was ending, and with that ending would go respect for herself. Only so long as mortals appreciated the freedom and beauty of the wild as a symbol of their joy in Earth would they appreciate her. She chose to leave before open disrespect began. Because you are the last of her line, the only child like her, she stopped time for a moment so that you might see her go. One last time."

The words were a whispered echo. Tears glistened in Medea's eyes, the grief of a child left behind.

"You will be the last to rule this land as it should be ruled. But before that can be—"

The priestess wrapped in the bearskin groaned and stirred, then coughed and came awake. She threw off the fur and sat up, wild-haired and then wide-eyed at the sight of Circe. Circe merely glanced her way, and the woman's eyes closed; her body went limp and sagged to the floor. The fur obligingly came to life and crept back to cover her.

"Someday you will understand why this pretense was necessary," Circe went on as if nothing had happened, "but then as now you will keep your knowledge to yourself. Mystery—not reality—is what mortals can accept and want to believe." The sweep of her arm took in the chamber and all within it.

Medea stared up at her. "*Are* you a witch?" she asked incautiously.

At that Circe's eyes narrowed and in the wavering light smoldered dark green like a dying wolf's. Her form seemed to grow more awesome. "Did Aeetes call me that?"

The little girl nodded, finally intimidated by this hint of lethal rage.

"In his round vanity he hopes to diminish me? Dismiss my power by giving me a petty label?" From the forest outside came the death cry of a rabbit. The night went still, as did Circe, who turned and stared into the darkness, as if she could see through it. When she turned back again, her face had softened. "Rabbits, like humans, possess a touching fear of death out of all proportion to their own importance." She smiled, as if to reassure her listener.

"I am the Enchantress—to use the kindest name men call me. Because your mother wishes it, I will be your teacher. But not until you're older. If I taught you now, you would become not my pupil but my thrall, a poor thing lacking will and judgment—and thus no credit to me. When I come again, you will know me by the falcon, the bird who is my eyes and spirit, the only creature whom I trust to call my one true name."

A lion coughed close by. Medea turned to see a black-maned male coming in the door, a rabbit dangling from its jaws. Circe spoke and the lion stopped and looked at her, eyes shining red in the light. She spoke again, words Medea couldn't understand, but the lion gave an almost human sigh, turned, and padded off into the night.

Medea watched it go; she'd never seen a lion so close up, never known they would come so near the city. And she had been outside alone. She turned to question Circe, but Circe had disappeared.

TWO

SHE LAY ON THE MOSSY LEDGE, chin on hands, unmoving. She was beautiful, as all of her mother's family had been. Her hair looked blue black, and her hazel eyes glowed green in the leaf-muted light. Her nose was elegant, her mouth well shaped, and her face shadowed by sadness, as if she knew too much for her age. She was ten years old.

She was hiding. All of the palace women had come berrying, and she had come along, not because she wanted to but because her stepmother and sister had insisted. It was her duty, they said, part of being gracious, of being who and what she was. A princess could not always remain a hoyden, running wild, doing only as she wished. "Especially at your age," Chalciope reminded her. "One stops being a child at seven."

And so Medea had slowed her steps and listened politely as the women spoke of husbands and lovers, pregnancy and servants—all of which she found tiresome. The only talk more boring was that of men telling endless hunting stories or reliving some old battle. At the first chance she had slipped away into the inhuman peace of the forest.

A wood thrush singing deep in the thicket reminded her of her mother's voice. She did not truly miss her mother, not anymore, but she missed a presence in the palace. When Asterodeia went away, the nightingales stopped singing in the courtyards. And no one filled jars with armloads of orange lilies or yellow mountain roses brought back from a morning ride. The palace air seemed denser, the walls more confining. The cool breezes that had drifted through the rooms on stifling summer nights no longer came.

She remembered Asterodeia, willow slender, with great dark eyes and a stillness in her soul, not much given to speech but the possessor of a soft, melodic voice heard always at a distance, like a haunting echo. She knew her stepmother, Eidyia, better than she had ever known her mother—but perhaps there was less to know. Where Asterodeia had been mystery and wild, half-understood charm, Eidyia was rosy-cheeked pragmatism, logic and kindness, a woman who made an effort to be good to her young stepdaughter, to give her as much attention as she gave her own infant son, Apsyrtus.

A noise startled her from her half doze in the sun, a stealthy *chink* of rock on rock, a *thinking* noise. As she sat up to listen, the birds stopped singing, and the hair rose on her arms. Without being able to see where or what it could be, she felt a hunter stalking her. The sheltered ledge was suddenly a trap, the walls blocking both view and escape. Not wanting to show fear and thus encourage attack, she got up slowly and pushed back her hair, then pretended to adjust her belt. In doing so, she unsheathed her dagger, keeping her hand concealed by the cloth blousing over her waist.

A dry branch snapped; her glance followed the sound. A man with a spear was crouching in the elder bushes just below the ledge. He was filthy, hairy, and wore only a raw deerskin, the forelegs knotted over one shoulder. A stone fetish hung on a thong around his neck; a waist thong held a canteen made from a deer bladder.

Although she'd never seen one alive before, she knew he was a mountain man, one of the remnants of an older race who lived in caves or crude huts high in the mountains. They existed by hunting, preying off shepherds' flocks, stealing from fields and orchards. It was said they stole children to use as slaves or meat. When they grew too bold, they were hunted down like any predator, their bodies brought back as trophies tied over the back of a horse.

A breeze wafted the smell of him to her, a mixture of sweat and the rotting rawhide. His eyes were an oily brown, the whites yellowed and bloodshot. When she met his gaze, he hissed with a sudden intake of breath, then smiled like a wolf sure of its quarry. His expression held no malice, only cunning, as he pushed his way out of the brush and came toward her.

Using his spear as a staff, he climbed the tumbled rock with terrifying ease, his splayed and callused feet scratching on the stone. When he reached out to grab her arm and pull her to him, the downward slash of her knife made him cry out in surprise. He jerked his arm away and tried to grab her leg and throw her. She slashed again. This time the black obsidian blade removed a neat slice from his wrist. A tendon gleamed before blood welled over the blue white cord. Red spurted onto the green moss.

High overhead a falcon cried, and the man stumbled. His spear dropped with a clatter, the shaft bouncing over the stones. He lost his footing and fell, clutching his wrist, trying to stop the blood oozing between his brown fingers. The elder bushes snapped and rustled as he tumbled through their canopy.

She jumped down from the ledge, wanting only to get past him and away before he could get up, but he was gone. A wild pig lay in the bushes, its trotters twitching as if a butcher had given it a hard blow to the head. Even as she stopped to stare, the pig rolled over and managed to sit up, then scrambled to its feet. It took a few staggering steps, bewildered, then began to tremble. With its right foreleg it reached out toward the spear, then stopped and turned its head in a most unpiglike manner, eyes almost crossed, to stare at the bleeding leg. Then it seemed to be looking at its tusks—or trying to—as if it had never noticed them before. A fly landed on its pink snout, and the pig's ears flapped. A short, questioning grunt ended in an odd squeal, then silence.

The pig stood stock still, then looked up at her. It had to turn its head to focus with its left eye. Crumbs of soil and leaf bits clung to its jowls and chest. The sight of her seemed to terrify it. It jumped and fell onto its rump and scrambled up immediately, only to have its legs give way. For a moment the animal lay still, quaking, then awkwardly raised its wounded leg into its line of vision, as if wanting to make sure of the gash across the hock. The leg jerked in a spasm. Blood ran toward

Middlesex Middle School Library Darien, CT. 06820

the shoulder. Horrified comprehension crossed the pig's face. Its eyes rolled back to expose the whites, and with a despairing squeal its head flopped onto the leaves.

"He's fainted," a voice said, and Medea jumped nearly as high as the man–pig had. Circe stood in the shade of an oak, leaning against the trunk. "They often do." She looked dispassionately at the pig, then reached down to pull a burr from her green gown, rolling the seedcase between thumb and forefinger, feeling the bristly texture.

"He knows he was a man," Medea whispered, awed. "He *knows.*" She was unsure if she wanted to be sick or not. Hearing about enchantments was much more fun than seeing one happen.

Circe turned to her. "I have demeaned him, as he wanted to demean you," she said, "but I leave him the freedom you would have been denied."

Medea felt the need to sit and did so. Since that night in the temple long ago, she had stopped hoping for Circe to reappear, becoming convinced that seeing her had been the dream Lukka so repeatedly assured her it was. Perhaps this was also a dream, and she was asleep in the sun. She pinched her arm and flinched with pain, then looked up, frightened. Circe was beside her, gazing down at her with inhuman tenderness.

At Circe's touch, vision blurred; the forest sounds faded and Medea fell into a comfortable, muzzy state, as if floating in a warm sea. "Look down," came Circe's command. "Always be aware."

As suddenly and inexplicably as man had become pig, the forest appeared far below Medea, the tree canopy visible as green tufts and florets carpeting the lower mountains. She could see the villages, fields and orchards, the city, and the Dawn Palace solidly atop its hill. All things human appeared unimportant, insignificant scars on the vast body of Earth. Even the snow-capped mountains were diminished. Higher, and all evidence of humans faded. In this distanced state, she was aware only of Earth and Sea and Energy, yet was sure she could still feel the sun-warmed stone beneath her bare feet.

The muzziness cleared; she seemed to be on a forested island ringed by white-capped breakers, an island in the sea, solitary and serene. Circe's isle? Around her were sand and seashells. Sandpipers fed at the water's edge, running ahead of the foamy fingers of incoming waves, hurrying after the foam as the waves retreated.

Sometimes it seemed to her that she would spend weeks on Circe's island before awareness would alter and she would find herself again in Colchis, as she had that first time, standing on the goat path, staring into space, aware that a servant woman had been sent to find her and bring her back to rejoin the women as they returned to the palace.

It was as if she experienced waking dreams, anywhere and often, or as if time altered and was not a continuum; for no matter how much time she thought she spent with Circe, no one in the Dawn Palace was aware she'd been away.

"I will not teach you to enchant, not yet. Perhaps never," Circe had told her that first day. They were walking the beach below her palace. "I will give you the awareness and the magic that knowledge brings."

"Do they always remember they were men?" The

child in her was still preoccupied by the pig's enchantment.

"Who?"

"The pigs."

"Some do. Those never quit hoping they will be
changed back. Others adapt quickly to grunting and
rooting for their food. Some go mad."

"And the rest?"

"Die."

In the center of the island, almost hidden by the
great trees, Circe's palace was a warren of chambers,
passageways and secret rooms—how many Medea
never knew. Those she saw opened onto a terrace overlooking the sea. Their walls glowed with murals that
altered themselves daily, and the floors were carpeted
with what felt like warm moss. Her wicker couch was
soft with furs; her bed a net of woven gold suspended
from four cone-shaped stands of carved ebony. A pool
cut into the living rock served as her bath and was
sluiced by the artesian spring flowing up from under
the building.

Circe had few human servants, and those few never
spoke, although they still had their tongues. They had
passed beyond the need for words. She had nonhuman
servants, too. Restless lions paced the beaches. Wolves
and bears patrolled the forest. There were baboons to
weave and clean and serve; they had been trained in
Egypt, Circe said, and were as skilled as any human in
their tasks.

Other creatures lived there, too, things that sidled
through the passages with claws clicking on the floors,
dim shapes in the shadows, eyes shining red at the edge
of the torchlight. Medea never saw them clearly and,

since Circe never acknowledged their presence, was afraid to ask what they might be or what their purpose was.

The hall containing Circe's loom was a light and airy place. Because she had no need for sleep, she would weave the night away, sometimes singing to herself, sometimes to the stars. When Circe sang her wordless songs, all else hushed to listen. The wind went still and the waves subsided. Whales would surface offshore; now and then a plume of spray would reveal where they floated. Forest creatures gathered below the open terrace, pig and lion side by side, ignoring one another. Raptors left their snags to perch on the palace rooftop, cocking their heads to better hear the song.

The tapestry Circe wove was incredibly complex, the colors rich and vibrant, the pictures alive. Only after years of study could Medea begin to see the pattern in the cloth. Much later she came to understand its logic, and that understanding gave her comfort.

Sometimes at night when Medea watched unobserved, Circe looked worn and old beyond time—almost like the death hag Aeetes said she was. Her face then was all bone and silence as she bent above her work, especially so when she had to alter patterns, discarding bits onto the floor. The falling threads would flare like sparks, and some would glow until she trampled them out.

At dawn they would go walking, she and Circe, and her lessons would take place. Circe was most lovely then, renewed by morning, released from her chores. Her face glowed in the early light, and her voice was charming.

"The magic I will teach you," Circe promised at the

start, "won't be the ugliness imagined by men now and in time to come. True magic demands no incantations, no chants, no secret words of power. No senseless sounds hummed until the skull vibrates with absurdity. There will be no blood, no obeisance to goat-footed gods with shaggy loins. All that is crude and false at best and gives power through fear only. The magic I will teach you will be knowledge and the only pure joy—that of learning. One thing more."

Around Medea's neck she placed a blue white crystal suspended on a thin rope of woven gold. The natural facets of the gem flashed in the sunshine. "This stone was formed when Earth began. One perfect starlit key to all time past and to come. With it you will have knowledge of time, will learn to see past and future—for all but what affects you. With that knowledge you will learn to align and focus your own will, and by your will to control."

"Why can't I learn my own future—or control it?" said Medea.

"Because to know in advance the inevitable sorrow that occurs in any life would spoil your pleasure in daily living.

"You are the daughter of starlight, the granddaughter of the sun. Of the two, starlight is far older, far more powerful. The sun was born of the stars, and without them would never have been. Men claim the sun as their own god and say that it is male. . . ." She smiled to herself. "But then in time they will claim to be the true creative force, true mothers, and say that women are only vessels, containers to nourish their seed.

"People want enchantment, myth and magic. They

are as passive as lovers in their ignorance of reality and as greedy for thrills. Belief in the supernatural frees them from responsibility—what is *unnatural* is beyond their control. It is easier to say 'The gods are against me' or 'She is a witch' than to think and act. It is their laziness that will make your knowledge seem magic."

In the stillness of Circe's island Medea was taught: how a viper's venom cured as well as killed, how mushrooms could bring visions or death or simply make a fire flare, how willow bark cured fever, how ore became silver and coal became oil, which plants made women fertile or barren and which did the same for men. Leaf and flower, root and seed, mineral and metal, everything in nature became a lesson.

"In time people will say of you that you know all the drugs that grow on Earth," Circe said. "They will be wrong. . . . You'll know far more than that."

THREE

ON THE MORNING OF HER THIRTEENTH BIRTHDAY, Medea wakened at first light. Lukka brought her pheasant dipped in honey, bread, wine and figs, and she ate as the slave dressed her. The king had asked her to join him in inspecting the palace storerooms and treasury, an honor shown no one else. But then, she reasoned, that was only proper. She was Asterodeia's youngest daughter and, by the matriarchal laws of Colchis, heir to this land. Aeetes ruled in her name and would do so until she married and produced a daughter and heir. Then, she supposed, her father would return to Corinth. She would miss him.

She knew King Aeetes was fond of her; what she had yet to realize was that he loved her because she reminded him of himself. He found his daughter Chalciope as placid as a broodmare and his son Apsyrtus childishly preoccupied with ships and swords, but Medea had a mind like his. In spite of being female, she seemed to understand that while war might be necessary or profitable, in the long run it was trade and agriculture that made a kingdom mighty.

But most of all Aeetes treasured her because she truly listened when he talked. The older he became, the more he delighted in telling her of his youth. As the poor young king of Corinth, he had dared leave his land to the care of a regent, migrate to distant Colchis and marry an alien queen. Despite the fact that he had lived in Colchis twice as long as in Greece, he spoke the local language poorly and still called Corinth "home."

When he spoke of his past, he would watch his reflection in Medea's eyes and see himself as he wished to be, powerful, resourceful, respected—not simply the barbarian king who had usurped his wife's holdings. Sometimes he was glad that Asterodeia, who knew him for what he was and had been, was no longer present. First wives, like older sisters, tended to remember a man's past differently.

Only a few slaves were up and about when Medea crossed the still-dark courtyard. She had been told to meet him at the main gate at sunrise. Aeetes was late as usual. To pass the time, she climbed the steps to the guard walk that rimmed the palace wall and looked down. Directly below, six Corinthian guards stood waiting to escort the royal party. They had been talking as she climbed the steps but, at the sound of her footsteps, looked up and, seeing her, fell silent. She removed herself from their visible discomfort by walking to the far corner of the wall.

Mist hung above the river. A fleet of boats was tied up at the quay. Others rested on the mudbanks. To the north and east the first rays of the sun struck the towering snowcaps of the high Caucasus Mountains and made a crenellation of gold. The lower mountains were dark blue. Across the river orchards bloomed, the blossoms blending with the mist. The air smelled of flowers and woodsmoke that drifted up from the city.

Early as it was, there was traffic on the river road. A herd of sheep and goats was being driven along by a whistling shepherd boy. Sheep bells tonkled sweetly; goats bleated in protest.

From this distance the shepherd looked to be her age. He moved gracefully in his dark cloak. She wondered if he were married and, had he been a prince, would he want to marry her? For herself—not for her wealth. No one else seemed to want her. No one that she wanted, at any rate. She had refused two old kings and was almost past the age to marry, but no match had been made. Lukka said that young men were afraid of both her and her father—but especially of her reputation as a witch. Medea's healing powers, while much in demand, were now so great that they aroused suspicion. To know so much was unnatural and made men ill at ease. Only Circe could have taught her that much— so people whispered and believed.

Perhaps they would be more accepting after she had married and become their queen, she thought. As queen, she could establish schools to teach all who wished to learn to read and write—not just the scribes and tax collectors. And she would share some of the herbal lore Circe had taught her. She would build a medical college at Aea and bring physicians from Egypt to teach. Knowledge would lessen the fears that ignorance inspired. As queen, she would have the swamps drained, and eliminate the source of many fevers. In return for their husbands' labor in draining the swamps, she would give a parcel of that rich bottomland to the wife of each freeman, land their daughters could inherit and pass on to their children. And then she would have the road to the inland sea improved to increase trade with the East.

Distracted from her daydreams by the gabble of geese, she watched the black skein of a flock stringing out across the milky sky, endlessly calling to one another as they flew. Suddenly she wanted to go with them, to fly and see new lands where, like the birds, she could find a true equal, a mate for life. She sighed; there was little hope of that. Kings of a rank to suit her wealth usually looked like Aeetes, or worse.

She envied Chalciope's four sons, who had set off the week before, planning to sail to Greece and claim a large inheritance—wealth their father, Phrixus, said had been left him by his Boeotian mother, Nephele. Although their father had died several years before, King Aeetes had been reluctant to let them go. In their absence the Dawn Palace was much quieter. Too quiet. She was imagining years to come of such quiet when the king came out into the courtyard, talking as he walked. He was flanked by his chamberlain, Toas, and trailed by six accountants, who took notes as they walked.

"I want a tally of the gifts received by the Temple of Ares during the spring festival," she heard him saying, "before those greedy priests manage to hide them all. And see if your spies can determine the value of donations to the Goddess. Tax revenues were good, but the festival games cost more than we had budgeted for, and we should buy two more war elephants. There's no reason why the various shrines can't contribute something."

Without a pause in his monologue, Aeetes smiled and offered her his hand as she came down the steps. She carefully grasped his fingertips. The king wore several rings on each thumb and every finger, rings that hadn't been removed for so long that the flesh had swelled around them. There was no tool slim and sharp enough to snip the gold without cutting him. Three years before, an Egyptian physician had attempted to solve the problem by suggesting a strict diet. After three days of fasting, Aeetes had had the physician whipped, stripped of all possessions and sent home naked on the next caravan leaving the city. Since then, no one had dared to make suggestions. Painful though the rings might be, Aeetes liked them; people who wished to continue living did not squeeze his hands.

Trees and bushes concealed the caves honeycombing the hillside below the Dawn Palace. In the early morning light the thick-planked gates of their entrances were noticeable only by the faint cart tracks leading to them. The caves had been used ever since people first wandered into this valley; indeed, one cave had been the first palace. Replaced as dwellings, they had served as barns and now as part of the royal treasury. Once there had been passageways and tunnels linking these caves with the Temple of the Goddess, as well as with other forgotten shrines in the hills, but Aeetes had had all the back passages sealed off for security.

In the floors of the largest chambers, cisterns had been cut into the stone and lined with vitrified clay to store honey, wine, and olive oil. Wall racks held jars of special wines. Other rooms were filled with bales of lamb and kidskins, fleeces, felts, stacks of furs and cured hides. The scent of precious woods sweetened the air of one cave; salt and spices were stored in another.

For each room an accountant produced an inventory tablet listing the room's contents and value. The guards served as torchbearers. As the party went from cave to cave, sense of smell became dulled by the many different odors. In confined space, even tin and copper smelled, Medea noted, peering into ore bins. Her favorite cave held the store of dried herbs, flower petals and spices. There, too, were beeswax, musk pods, incense, a dozen different precious oils, opium, and perfumed unguents in tiny clay pots with wax-sealed lids. These goods were worth far more than their weight in gold. This cave, like the gold and gem room beneath the palace proper, was kept under armed guard.

Although the walking was often steep and difficult for a person of his age and bulk, Aeetes didn't seem to mind. Seeing his wealth made him smile more broadly with each stop. "When you have a palace of your own, never store oil and wine under your roof," he cautioned Medea. "If enemies attack, or a careless spark falls from a torch, all you own can go up in flame."

"When I have a palace of my own?" she said, thinking she had misunderstood.

"Yes."

"But the Dawn Palace is mine. It passes always to the youngest daughter."

"No more," Aeetes said bluntly. "It's mine. That was the price your mother agreed to pay for my protection. For my army. Without me, Colchis would be an Egyptian colony again. No. This land is mine, and by my law—Greek law—my son Apsyrtus will be my heir."

Had he looked at his daughter, he would have seen her go deathly pale. In that moment her face changed subtly, permanently, as if all trace of childhood's innocence had been erased. "And your kingdom—Corinth —in Greece? Is that Apsyrtus's too?"

"One third of Corinth will be yours. When you marry. And of course I will provide you with a dowry, a generous one." He broke the musk pod he had been nervously fingering and sniffed loudly. "Fine stuff," he said, as if hoping to distract her.

She stood in furious silence, shocked, trying to absorb this flood of dreadful understanding, this sudden death of her dreams of ruling Colchis, of being the best in a proud line of queens. Disinherited! By a half brother—and her mother's vulnerability. Disinherited. With no recourse. If she stayed here, if she did not marry, she would become a threat, tolerated by Aeetes for the air of legitimacy Asterodeia's offspring bore in the minds of the Colchian people. In time she would become the high priestess in the Temple of the Goddess—if he would allow that. But what real power would the temple have—what did it have now—if women and the matriarchy no longer ruled? None. None that mattered. And if Apsyrtus should come to power . . .

"In Corinth and in Thebes," Aeetes interrupted her thoughts, "some fear thieves more than fire and keep the oil inside." He met her eyes and saw her expression. "I thought you knew," he said then, almost gently, "that you would *assume,* when you weren't proclaimed queen after your mother passed from the living."

"I was an infant then. I thought—" A surge of grief, betrayal and loss caught like a pain in her chest, and she nearly doubled over. "I loved you!" she whispered. "I trusted you."

"And so you should. I am your father. Nothing has changed between us."

"Except your betrayal."

"I did not betray you—"

"But Circe said I would be queen."

"My witch sister has no power over me!" Aeetes' face went red with anger. "You are too young. You don't understand. I've done you no harm. Your mother did what she had to do. She had no army and no administrative sense. Pride and a sense of style only take you so far. If it hadn't been me, it would have been another king. Or several kings. Remember that! Toas! Come here! I want to hear the livestock count. All of it!"

Not wanting to give the eunuchs more to gossip and intrigue about, Medea turned away into the shadows until she had regained her self-control. She would think about this later, when she was alone.

Before approaching, Toas paused to consult one of the accountants, who handed the older man a book. Toas unrolled the scroll with a flourish and with a wealth of flowery phrases, began to read.

"In addition to the sacred six white stallions and six black mares, mighty Aeetes owns one hundred and twenty-five Cilician thoroughbreds, housed in the royal stables; seven hundred lesser horses in the hill pastures; three hundred head of fat cattle; ten thousand sheep and goats; two thousand asses, chiefly employed in the mines and quarries; ten war elephants . . ." He paused to consult the accountant and gave his lord and Medea a sideways glance before continuing. "And in the charge of the southern military governor, one hundred and ten of the Bactrian beasts used as pack animals to carry salts and naphtha from the inland sea."

Toas was beginning to list the flocks of peafowl, guineas, chickens, and doves when the king waved a beringed hand for silence and led the way to daylight.

All of this belonged to my mother and now none of it is mine, Medea thought as she followed him out. Why did he ask me to come with him? For company—or because he wanted to tell me this and knew no better way?

From the caves they visited the stables and barns, then went by chariot to inspect the flocks being readied for the move to summer pasture. A mild winter had resulted in a good lambing season which, added to the animals gained by the spring tax, had almost doubled the king's herds.

On the way back to the palace, Aeetes, again in good humor, gave Toas orders for a special feast that evening, "so that all the household may celebrate my wealth! We will have music and dancing. And prizes. People always perform better for a prize."

FOUR

To a certain extent we create the roles we play in life, our character based on what we think we are, our actions on how we wish others to see us. Medea had always assumed that she would be the queen of Colchis, perhaps the last of her line, if Circe was correct, but queen nonetheless. To learn that all she had assumed was hers would instead be her half brother's left her bewildered, unsure of how to act.

Late that afternoon she was on the roof terrace, combing her hair dry in the sun, her lyre on the floor beside her couch. Unable yet to face the enormity of change in her role, her mind sought refuge in the banal. Her thoughts alternated between cold, indignant rage and wondering if she had time to rehearse the song Aeetes had ordered her to sing that night. She decided she was too upset to sing; the last thing she needed today was humiliation if she performed poorly.

In the still air, the smell of baking bread and meats rose from the ovens at the end of the kitchen courtyard.

Somewhere within the palace the choir was rehearsing a new song poem, their part of the evening's entertainment. The choir from the Dawn Palace was renowned throughout Colchis and beyond, in all the towns and villages between Aea and Troy. The choir had won more competitions than any in remembered history, and won honestly.

She had just put down her comb and stretched out on the felted couch to listen when someone began shouting down by the quay. Ignoring the shouts, she concentrated on the high, sweet tenor solo Toas was singing. That such a pure voice should issue from that fussy martinet always fascinated her. The shouting came closer. Dogs began to bark. The singing broke off abruptly, followed by a burst of excited chatter from the central courtyard. With a sigh, she rose and went to look over the wall to see what the commotion was about.

A young barbarian was striding up the road. His long, curly hair was sunbleached to the color of pale straw; his beard was reddish gold. Clad in a scarred leather tunic and a nearly bald lion skin, he had the body of a galley slave, oiled and well muscled. He carried an ornate brass shield, indicating a warrior's noble rank, but bore no other weapons, suggesting that he came in peace. Other men were trailing behind him, as if he were their leader—although they wore Colchian dress.

Suddenly Chalciope came out of the gate and ran down the steps. She went directly to the men following the stranger—behavior that at any other time Medea would have found curious as well as rude. Now she was only vaguely aware of Chalciope, being preoccupied. The young barbarian was the most handsome man she'd ever seen.

In the shade of the giant beech trees at the top of the hill, he stopped to rest from the climb and stood looking up at the shining palace. He turned in a slow circle to admire the view and began to smile, slowly, as if immensely pleased by what he saw. His teeth flashed white in his sunbrowned face. In sudden empathy, she saw what he viewed for the first time: the fountains; the rows of blooming trees; the palace gleaming a pale pinkish white amid the pines and oaks; the hills around; the high, blue mountains in the background. Travelers all said that the Dawn Palace was the most beautiful in the world.

Behind him Chalciope embraced one man, then another, and Medea belatedly realized they were her sister's sons—supposedly on their way to Greece. Before she could wonder why they had returned so quickly, and in the company of this barbarian, a trumpet sounded. The king and queen were coming out to greet the visitors. Her sons were presenting the stranger to Chalciope now, and she seemed to be thanking him for something.

Medea wrapped a gold cord around her still-damp hair and ran down the stairs to the inner courtyard. She had to push her way through a cluster of curious servants at the gate. From inside the courtyard she could hear Aeetes shouting in anger—something he never did.

"Don't tell me you're heir to that throne and expect me to be impressed," Aeetes was yelling as Medea came down the terrace steps. "I know that country! A noble is any man who owns three sheep and a goat! If he's lucky enough to steal another man's horse, he calls himself king! A palace there is any hut where you can't smell the midden while you eat."

The young man answered so softly that Medea couldn't hear his reply, but whatever he said only made Aeetes angrier.

"You come here with a ship and crew that size—which you take pains to hide from view—and you think I won't guess your real motives? You want the trade of the coastal towns! You want the riches of Colchis! Go back where you came from before I have your lying tongue cut out and your thieving hands cut off!"

"I am neither merchant nor thief, mighty Aeetes," the stranger said as Medea slipped by Toas to stand beside her father. "My mission here is sacred—" His eyes met Medea's and he fell silent, then began to smile again.

He smelled of worn leather and the sea and sunshine on crushed wild mustard plants. He smelled too of sweat: fish had obviously been his main diet for weeks, and wine—crude, raw wine unsweetened by honey. There was no scent of fear.

She looked into those gentle, lazy, smiling hazel eyes and knew that she had always missed the laughter and the careless ease they promised. Her glance slid to his soft mouth and she longed to kiss him, to feel his arms close round her. All thought, all logic left her mind then; her years of study, of learning, her position as a priestess of the Goddess, her desire to rule her mother's land—all faded from importance. All that mattered was this man. She felt her will dissolve, as if she had been possessed by a strange presence.

"My daughter, Medea."

The too-long silence, of which she had not been aware, was broken by her father's grudging introduction.

"Medea! All they say is true. You are as lovely as a goddess!" The young man raised his shield in salute. "I am Diomedes, the son of Aeson, heir to the throne of Iolcus. My foster father always called me Jason. Out of respect for him, I prefer that name."

"Why are you here?" she asked in her direct manner.

"He's come to desecrate the Grove of Ares," the king said before the younger man could speak. "At least that's his excuse."

Jason gave him a puzzled stare, as if trying to imagine what he had done to provoke such ire. When he finally spoke again, he addressed himself to Medea alone. "I'm here on a sacred mission. Years ago, through treachery, my father lost his throne to King Pelias, who imprisoned my parents in their own palace. He would have killed them, but he loved my mother and he was afraid she would die of grief if he killed my father. She was pregnant at the time, and I was born shortly after. Knowing Pelias would kill me—or any rightful heir—my mother pretended I had died at birth. She had her women wail and lament, and she herself wrapped me in linen like a loaf of shepherd's bread and had me smuggled out of the palace. I was taken to the hills, to live on Mt. Pelion with Chiron, the centaur, my foster father. He raised me to manhood."

[*49*]

Jason paused, disconcerted by the intensity with which Medea was studying his face as he spoke. "It's a complicated story. Worthy of one of the songs your people sing. But what you must understand and believe is that, before I can restore the Iolcan throne to my father, before King Pelias will relinquish his claims, Iolcus must be freed from a curse."

"That of poverty, no doubt," growled Aeetes.

Jason cast his lazy glance at the king. "That's true, mighty Aeetes. And worse. Much worse." He turned to Chalciope. "Your husband, Prince Phrixus, found refuge here in Colchis when he and his sister Helle took the fleece of the Sacred Ram. As you know, both had been dedicated as their father's sacrifice to the ram god. Not willing to die for him, they fled. Ever since, because they were cheated of what should have been theirs, the gods have sent plagues and droughts to punish Iolcus. Then, when Phrixus died here, he was denied a proper Greek burial. His ghost haunts us at home." Jason's eyes clouded with memory.

"His body was treated with all honor," said Chalciope, worried. "It was wrapped in a fine oxhide and placed in the top of the tallest beech tree in the Valley of the Dead. Colchian custom forbids the burial of men's bodies, as they profane Earth the Mother," she explained, "and cremation is forbidden by those who worship fire."

"I consulted the oracle at Delphi," said Jason. "The oracle said that Iolcus will never prosper until Phrixus's ghost is at rest. His bones must be buried in Greek soil. The sacred Golden Fleece must be returned to its shrine. To do this, all the kingdoms of Greece have sac-

[50]

rificed to build the world's finest ship, the *Argo*. King Pelias himself contributed the most—"

"To get rid of you, obviously," Aeetes interjected.

"So it would seem to the cynical," said Jason, "but to prove his good faith, King Pelias sent his son and heir, Acastus, along on the quest. He is aboard the *Argo* now, along with the other heroes chosen as its crew. I am the captain. Only by the help of the gods have we reached Colchis. We beg you not to cause our sacrifice to have been in vain. We beg you to give us the bones and the Fleece that hold Phrixus's soul to this land so that we may return both to their proper home. Surely, madam, you wish rest for your husband's spirit?"

"I didn't know he—"

Aeetes interrupted. "Surely, Greek, you can't expect me to believe you have come all this way for bones and a fleece, no matter how sacred?"

"He saved our lives, Grandfather." Melanion, Chalciope's eldest son, spoke up. "When our ship capsized in the storm, everyone was drowned but us. We clung to the wreckage and were washed ashore more dead than alive. Luckily Jason and the Argonauts were camped for the night on that island. They pulled us out of the water, fed us, gave us clothing—and brought us home. If Jason had dishonorable intentions, he could have killed us there."

"And waste four guides and the perfect introduction to me and your mother?" Aeetes' laughter contained no trace of amusement. "You were a gift from the gods, you stupid boy."

"Sure proof then that the gods favor me," Jason said but was ignored.

"We knew you'd be angry, sir, when you heard the favor he asks." Argeus, the favorite grandson, came forward. "But you might weigh the fact that Jason is our blood kin, our cousin. His grandfather, Cretheus, was brother to our father's father, Athamas the Mighty."

"Since Athamas died a madman and Cretheus' son Aeson was too weak to hold his kingdom for his son—who stands here before me begging favors—your kinship doesn't impress me. Nor should it you," said Aeetes. He frowned as another thought came to him: "How did you get past the Trojan ships that guard the entrance to the Black Sea?"

Jason shrugged. "I'd like to say that we defeated them in a glorious battle, but the truth is, no one tried to stop us."

"No one?"

"No one."

The king's already high color deepened with added displeasure. In return for a large annual tribute from himself, Troy was to keep adventurers such as Jason from ever entering the Black Sea, thus limiting trading competition as well as pirate raids on the coastal towns. Troy had always lived up to its side of the bargain. Thus, either Jason was lying, or his ship was so large and well armed that Trojan patrol boats feared to stop it. Or had Troy fallen? A city so rich attracted too many enemies.

The king turned to his grandsons. "We'll talk privately. Come." He turned to the gate, then turned back to his guards as an afterthought. "The Greek will be our guest tonight. See that no moment passes during which he lacks your utmost attention."

Twilight fell. Braziers smoked atop tall tripods. On their glowing coals aromatic roots had been sprinkled so that the scents repelled biting flies and mosquitoes. Dozens of lamps added their smoke to the insect-repellent effort.

In the terraced courtyard, noble diners reclined on narrow couches. Beside each couch was a low table. On the highest terrace, on thronelike chairs, sat the king and queen and their young son, Apsyrtus. The royal table was especially beautiful, made of ebony inlaid with crystals and mother-of-pearl, with elegant legs shaped like a fawn's with golden hooves.

Servants carrying heavy trays moved among the diners. The menu for the feast included honey-glazed songbirds stuffed with barley, to be eaten whole, the fragile bones crushed and swallowed. There was pheasant stuffed with dried figs; lamb grilled over charcoal; kid roasted with lemon and garlic; squash baked with sliced apples and honey; bowls of lettuces, radishes, leeks, and green onions; loaves of bread to wipe juices from one's hands and mouth.

Bones, fat, gristle, anything unwanted was dropped on the ground to be raked away later or buried under a fresh layer of river sand. On humid days no amount of aromatic herbs could mask the faint but pervasive rancidness of this courtyard.

On the lowest terrace, tubbed pines outlined a stage. Behind the trees musicians played. A wild-eyed juggler entertained court children by doing tricks with brass hoops. When the music stopped, the noise level of conversation fell and the cheerful noise of the servants' feast could be heard from the kitchen courtyard. Those serving the royal guests cast longing glances toward the wall; a feast for all meant all but those who served the feast.

Medea sat one level below the king. She wore a gown of blue Egyptian cotton, finely pleated and formfitting with a bodice that both cradled and exposed her breasts. A filmy capelet, gold-clasped at the throat, covered her magnificent shoulders. Heavy gold gleamed from her waist, wrists, arms and ankles; more gold was braided through her hair. She rather dimmed her sister Chalciope, who sat next to her, dressed in a plain white linen gown, deep in conversation with her sons, who were seated on the next level down with their guest.

Jason lounged sideways on his couch, his face in half profile—his most becoming pose. "You're eating little and talking less," he said, nodding at Medea's plate of untouched food.

She smiled, unable to explain that she could not eat and could scarcely think for wanting him. Her nephews had provided him with a dress tunic of blue kid embroidered with gold lions, and an ivory kiltlike skirt. On his wrists were wide golden cuffs, which she recognized as Melanion's. Bathed and oiled, with hair and beard neatly trimmed, he looked far more like a prince. But, in a way, she thought, she'd liked his wild, unkempt beauty more. Neatness somehow diminished him.

"I notice you don't eat anything that Melanion hasn't tasted first," she said. "Do you fear being poisoned?"

"No. I fear making a fool of myself." He grinned at his own honesty. "Most of this food is strange to me. I don't know how to eat it."

"You don't have lettuce in Iolcus?" She pointed to the leafy head he had discreetly dropped on the ground beneath his table.

"That? That's horse food."

"And the lamb with lemon. Or the pheasant? Neither pleases you?"

"Oh, no. Both do. What it is . . . I'm uncomfortable sitting here in luxury while my crew camps in the river mud—"

"You can set your mind at ease." Aeetes had obviously been listening and now interrupted. "As a good host to heroes on a sacred quest, I've given orders to have my soldiers escort your men and ship here to Aea to be tied up to the quay. That way we can all view this wonder, the *Argo,* and there'll be no danger of any of your heroes getting lost in the swamps . . . should they try to find their way to the Sacred Fleece in the dark."

With the deliberateness of a sybarite, Aeetes rolled two perfect lettuce leaves into a cone and filled the hollow with shreds of lamb and chives. "I told my men to make sure all your heroes remained on board the *Argo.* It would be a shame if any missed our hospitality." The gems in his rings flashed as he bit into the lettuce.

"You are gracious, mighty Aeetes." Jason's face was impassive.

"Always." Aeetes pointed toward the stage with his lettuce cone. "Our choir. You'll enjoy this, prince of Iolcus. We have excellent musicians."

Jason didn't even glance at the brightly robed figures filing onto the stage. "Have you decided to give me the Sacred Fleece?"

Aeetes' crown shivered and chimed as he moved. "My decision can keep until we've heard the singing." He nodded to the choirmaster that the music might begin.

The song told of a mountain nymph who passed her carefree days playing musical stones by striking them with an ibex horn. As she wandered through the wild, her music attracted a hunter. Tantalized, forgetting both prey and duty, he followed the nymph, day and night, summer and autumn, always seeking the joy her music promised.

Toas sang the narrator's role; a contralto was the hunter; the unseen nymph was a flute, and her music was the choir. The music of the lyres depicted the wind and rain and, as the hunter, still obsessed, died of starvation, the cold purity of falling snow.

Medea watched the evening star sink behind the wall. Although the sun had long since set, the snow on the peaks of the Caucasus still fired blood red in the last rays. Bats flew above the courtyard, darting as quickly as her thoughts: Granted Aeetes was greedy and judged all men by his own standards—was he right about this beautiful Greek? Why should that weather-ruined fleece be so important to Jason's gods? And if Phrixus's ghost was here, how could they know that in Iolcus, or Delphi? If the ghost roamed all the way to Greece, why couldn't they find a way to keep it there? Why would they need a special ship to carry home bones and a fleece? She wished she could discuss it all with Circe; Circe had little patience with male spiritual pretensions.

Night had fallen by the time the music ended. In the brief silence, the frog chorus could be heard. In the hills, hyenas barked and an aurochs bawled, possibly for the death of her calf. The king sat wiping away his tears and vigorously blew his nose. He could watch a man being flayed to death without a qualm, but choral music always made him sob, as did trumpet fanfares or the drumbeat of his army going off to war.

Conversation broke out again. There was movement among the guests. Servants bustled about, clearing away bowls and platters and bones, bringing in sweet cakes, fruits, and more wine. The queen's women distributed gifts and praise to the musicians for their performance.

When order was more or less restored, the king called for silence. He was going to make a speech. He thanked the entire serving staff and cooks, the choir, musicians, and entertainers. He thanked his father and the various gods and goddesses for a season of such bounty. No one was ignored.

As the speech droned on, Jason grew visibly impatient. Aeetes stopped and fixed him with a stare that went on for so long that all eyes turned to the young man. "A great hero has been our guest tonight," the king said then, turning to the crowd. "He is one of fifty heroes, all so bold and brave that they felt the need to hide their ship in a backwater in order not to frighten us by their arrival. They were being so considerate because they seek a favor, the Sacred Fleece brought here by Phrixus.

"In memory of my homeland, and because my grandsons have returned safely, I will grant this favor—on these conditions: Prince Jason must yoke the bulls of Hephaestus and plow the Field of Ares."

Exclamations of surprise and disbelieving laughter

[57]

broke out among the guests. Aeetes ignored them. "When the field is plowed," the king went on, "he must sow it with the serpent's teeth he is said to carry with him—given to him by Athena. If he can harvest the crop that grows from those seeds, he can take the Sacred Golden Fleece and the bones of Phrixus back to Greece." Then, looking at Jason again, the king asked: "Do you accept this challenge?"

A mocking little night wind played with Jason's hair. He sat stiffly erect, as if stunned by what was asked of him. Beyond the courtyard walls the frogs and insects sang, indifferent to human affairs, intent on their own short lives.

"Well?" prompted Aeetes when the silence had gone on too long.

Jason seemed to become aware of him and his audience then and sprang quickly to his feet. "I accept your challenge."

Scattered whoops of excitement escaped from some of the young men, but the elders looked troubled and whispered among themselves. Without a word, Eidyia rose and hurried from the courtyard, followed by her women. Medea looked from Jason's face, pale with determination, to her father's. Aeetes was flushed with satisfaction, as if he'd just come from a victory or a particularly exciting couch.

Anger rose like bile in her throat, and she knew she had to get away. Not caring that it was against protocol to leave before the king, not caring how undignified she looked, she ran out, dodging couches and tables, brushing against serving people.

"Medea!" Chalciope called after her. "Medea! Wait!"

Medea didn't stop until she had reached the quiet of Asterodeia's deserted courtyard. Breathless, she sat down on a bench and looked up at the stars, trying to regain her sense of perspective.

"Sister?" came Chalciope's voice. "Please. I must talk with you. Are you ill?"

"No!" Couldn't the fool see she wanted to be left alone?

"Good. Because you must talk with Father. You're his favorite. You must make him understand. This trial he's set for Jason is a mistake. There is no reason for it. Phrixus's bones *should* be buried; his beliefs weren't ours. And as for the Golden Fleece, it's being kept in Colchis purely out of spite. I can't believe the All-Powerful Mother cares what becomes of such a worthless relic. But if Jason dies for it—and you know he will—his friends may feel they must avenge his death. Then others will die. My sons are with the Greeks now, you know, and may be the next to die—if only because they're close at hand. You must ask Father to stop this, beg him if you must!"

"No," said Medea. "Not in this. You saw his face tonight. You know how stubborn he is. . . ." Suddenly she doubled over with pain, imagining Jason dead. "He can't die!" she blurted. "I won't let him! I love him!"

"Oh, my dear." Murmuring her concern, Chalciope sank down beside her sister and attempted to comfort her. "You can't mean Jason? To love him would be unwise—a most inappropriate passion."

"Inappropriate? Would it be more appropriate for me never to marry—as my father would prefer? Or to marry one of those old men Eidyia favors for me? I want Jason. I'm going to help him win the Fleece—and lay Phrixus's ghost to rest. And when the *Argo* sails, I'm going with him to be his wife and queen!"

"But how can you—"

"You're going to help me. Now listen."

FIVE

MIDNIGHT HAD COME AND GONE. The lamplight flickering over the painted horses on the wall made their wild eyes gleam. The warm room smelled of herbs laced with something acrid. With the shutters closed and the wind drapes drawn and her world reduced to this room, Medea sat on a three-legged stool beside her workbench, her bare feet resting on a rung, her elbows on the bench top. She was still wearing the gown she'd worn at the feast.

The bench lamp burned to heat the bulb of a long-necked glass vessel clamped to a tripod. Silvery bubbles rose in the vessel's amber liquid and broke to dew the glass throat. A small jar and cork stopper lay to one side.

To her right on the bench top was a small black chest, intricately carved and shiny with age. The twin lids of the chest were winged open to reveal, snugly fitted into padded hollows like a collection of precious bibelots, bottles and vials and jars cut from gemstone, each with a stopper topped by a gemstone cabochon and identified by a gold tag on a fine gold chain. Far more precious than the containers were the liquids inside.

As she watched the vessel simmer, waiting for the heat to turn the amber liquid dark red, she cupped her chin on her hands and was shocked to find her fingers were ice cold while her face felt feverish. The symptoms went with the fatigue that made her head feel too heavy for her neck. This passion for Jason was like an illness, she thought resentfully. Was what was called love nothing but symptoms—pulse whispering in ears, cold hands, tremors, shortness of breath, vertigo at the thought of his touch? If so, then love was a weakness, a vulnerability, a thing to be concealed.

What if he refused her offer? What if he was determined to win the Sacred Fleece all by himself? What if he merely thought she was pretty but didn't want her as a wife? What if her nephews had talked too much about her powers? What if he loved someone else? What would she do with this love she felt for him? The thought of losing him was too painful to consider.

Chalciope had called her love an inappropriate passion. But why was her passion less appropriate than her sister's loveless marriage and mating with Phrixus? Phrixus, who even as a ghost apparently refused to take responsibility for himself and drifted from place to place, sighing. She smiled to herself, thinking that Circe was right; souls were what they were from birth to death and beyond, in any stage, shape, or time. All one had to do was learn to see the true shape of a creature's spirit.

Because he had died when she was an infant, she could only dimly remember Phrixus, a timid man who never understood why he should have lived while his sister drowned on their fateful trip to Colchis, who used to wake the palace with his nightmares of being a sacrificial victim. According to the slaves' gossip, he was worthless as a warrior, freezing with fear at the enemy's first battle cry. No wonder Aeetes had let him stay and marry his eldest daughter; prince though he was, and son of a mighty king, Phrixus had been no threat to Aeetes' crown. Until now.

At the sound of footsteps and whispering in the next room, Medea reached over and closed the wooden chest. When it was shut, no clasps or hinges showed; the box looked like an ancient wooden headrest, or simply a decorative piece. The liquid in the glass had turned red. Moving the jar into position, she tilted the flask with her wooden tongs and poured. The jar was still steaming when she put the cork in.

When the door opened, her heart skipped a beat and she involuntarily held her breath—only to see Chalciope push aside the wind drape.

"He's waiting outside."

"Will he marry me?"

"He seems more than eager to do so. But are you sure—?" Seeing Medea's resolute expression, Chalciope sighed, then shook her head. "Medea, think. You are making yourself completely vulnerable. Even if he is successful in his quest and the kingdom of Iolcus becomes his, Iolcus is a poor place. You may be learned and powerful, but if he betrays you, where will you go? What will you do? You'll be far from home. Father will never forgive you. His allies won't be allowed to help you. What will you do?" she repeated.

"Jason won't betray me," Medea stubbornly insisted. "Why would he? My love can only be of benefit to him."

Chalciope studied her sister's face, as if seeing her for the last time, then reached out and gently stroked Medea's cheek. "So be it," was all she said.

To hide the fact that she was shaking with excitement, Medea put on a soft woolen cape that covered her from head to foot, then, just in case he might still be able to see her trembling, she blew out two of the lamps, leaving only the coals in the fire pit and the bench lamp as light.

Chalciope returned almost immediately with Jason. Medea was standing beside the table, leaning against it to control her shaking. As chaperone, the elder sister seated herself on the couch nearest the door.

Jason paused, as if to orient himself in the gloom, or to assure himself that he hadn't walked into a trap. When he saw that only Medea was there, a tender smile lit his whole face—and with that smile she felt her tension melt away. He came toward her, reached out almost shyly and took her cold hands in his. Their eyes met and she was sure his face reflected the same love she felt for him.

And when he leaned closer and gently, chastely, kissed her lips and eyes and forehead, she was completely sure.

"What a priceless gift you offer me, Princess," he whispered then. "Once, long ago and far away, an oracle promised that love would find me here, but I didn't believe. And even when I saw you and wished that you were mine, I did not dare to hope that promise could come true. Has it, or am I dreaming of you in this warm darkness?"

In reply, she cupped his face in her hands and kissed him in return. "It's true," she said and put her arms around his neck. She felt weak with relief and tenderness. He loved her!

They stood clasped in an embrace until Chalciope coughed discreetly to remind them she was there. Slowly, reluctantly, both faces turned toward her.

"Forgive my intrusion," she said, "but in my role as go-between—and in spite of what I witness—I feel I must make sure that you, Jason, understand the bargain between yourself and Princess Medea."

"I do."

"And what do you understand?"

He thought for a moment before smiling his easy smile. "Why, that she makes no bargain at all, but an outright gift to me. I understand that she will, by her special talents, ensure my success in the trials that King Aeetes plans for me. In return, I will marry her and make her my queen." His face softened again as he looked at the girl in his arms. "Oh, Medea, to have you as my bride will be a gift for which I will never cease to sacrifice to the gods in gratitude. I swear it!"

As if suddenly inspired, he slipped out of the embrace and raised his right arm to the hidden sky. "I swear by mighty Zeus, and by Mother Hera, and by all the gods of Olympus, to keep faith with Medea *forever*. I swear that if she will be my wife, I will forever love, cherish, and protect her. And should I ever forsake her, or cause her grief or harm, may you punish me as I shall deserve to be punished! This is my sacred oath!"

She thought his eyes had filled with tears, but in the dim light couldn't be sure. More important, she felt the same powerful presence she had experienced that afternoon when they first met. It had entered the room as he invoked his alien gods. The presence was not frightening or disapproving, but simply there, watching. If Jason felt it, he gave no external sign, but from the corner of her eye Medea saw Chalciope stand and peer uneasily into the shadows, as if she too suspected something beside themselves had borne witness to Jason's oath.

What Aeetes so grandly called the Field of Ares was the meadow used as a practice field by his army. Between the soldiers' training sessions, goats kept the grass clipped short, a useful service in this wet climate. Located in a valley below the palace, the field was bordered by stone barracks, pine woods, and a rocky stream where icy mountain water rushed to meet the rivers.

The morning was fine and cool, and most of the townspeople had come out to enjoy the spectacle. Benches had been erected during the night. All the seats were taken by daybreak. Latecomers milled about or gathered in small groups to talk. Behind the gallery, slaves hunched over braziers, grilling meats impaled on sticks. Others unpacked baskets of bread, cheese, fruit and wine so that their masters might breakfast. Cooking smells and charcoal smoke drifted toward the river. Aeetes' warriors lined the riverbank, guarding the *Argo* and her crew, brought there during the night. Children raced about excitedly, their voices as shrill as the gulls that floated overhead, waiting for scraps. The occasion had the air of an impromptu holiday.

When Medea arrived with the rest of the royal retinue, she saw Jason waiting at the edge of the field. With him stood Chalciope's sons, still loyal to the man who had saved their lives. From the vantage point of the reviewing stand, she could see that people avoided looking at the five young men, as they would avoid staring at any ill-omened thing. It was then that she first noticed the *Argo* and understood her father's unease.

It was a thirty-oared warship, sleek and narrow, with a ram's head on the prow. Below the ram's head, on either side, was a large, staring eye in white and green with black lashes. The red of the sail, now furled, matched the worn red of the sides. A wicker frame supported a hide roof to keep the rain off the oarsmen. A platform gave the helmsman a clear view over the roof. She'd seen larger, more impressive ships, merchant vessels from Canaan and Egypt, but none that looked quite so ferocious. She looked back again at Jason, studying him in light of this ship.

Dressed again in his worn tunic and lion skin, armed with shield, spear and sword, he looked the barbarian warrior he was. His skin glowed pink with the potion she'd brewed the night before. Stains on his shield indicated he'd rubbed the liquid on the metal. She wondered why—perhaps he thought the drug was magic, a liquid shield of power?

King Aeetes settled heavily onto the royal bench beside her and tugged his gold-trimmed white robe over his skinny knees. As the sun's first rays came over the mountains and struck the Dawn Palace, he gave the signal for the trials to begin. Trumpets sounded a fanfare. The crowd hushed. In the sudden quiet, they could hear the trumpets echoing back from the hills. From the river came the faint sound of ducks quacking, an oddly homey touch.

The bulls of Hephaestus were kept locked and guarded in a stone stable next to the armory, tended by their own private blacksmith and a keeper, the positions handed down from generation to generation.

There were shouts from the crowd, and Medea turned to see the massive stable doors slowly swinging open. Thick black smoke billowed out, and a sulfurous, tarry stench filled the cool air. First one and then the other bull appeared and lumbered down the earthen ramp. Each hoof left a deep imprint in the hard-packed ground. The crowd went still again, as did the birds.

The bulls were huge and black and gleaming in the sunlight. Their hooves, tails and curved horns were brass. Heavier than an aurochs and more barrel-chested, they moved at an ominous pace. Their legs were short and massive, the joints bending as no mortal animal's bent. Their great heads nodded up and down, spurting smoke and steam from ears and flaring nostrils. Every few steps they took a fierce breath, and their eyes rolled and glowed red with a deep inner fire. Above the hiss of their breathing could be heard a rhythmic throb and small screeches that suggested they suffered endless pain. These sounds seemed to unnerve the crowd more than the bulls' appearance. As the creatures advanced inexorably across the field, the spectators began to back away, and some turned and ran in panic.

Medea looked over at Jason, who appeared calm. He saluted the brothers as they left him to face this challenge, then laid down his shield and weapons to signify his readiness.

"Bring on the yoke and plow!" Aeetes ordered.

Two men hurriedly lugged a black metal ox yoke out onto the field. Two others brought a black plow. Both pieces were brass-trimmed, like the bulls.

Medea had never seen the bulls before; she had only heard about them. Aeetes kept them so well hidden that they appeared perhaps once in a lifetime, like the great comet, and inspired similar terror and superstitions. She had expected them to be clever automatons, walking statues propelled by slaves hidden inside, but there was nothing human inside these fiery things. Their size and power filled her with dread. The drug she'd given Jason bestowed unnatural strength and protection from fear, but it would never enable him to stop these creations, let alone yoke and plow the field with them.

As Jason picked up the yoke and walked to intercept them, it became clear that the bulls were a head taller than he and that if one stepped on him, or gored him, or breathed on him, he would die. In spite of their fear, the crowd moved closer.

Medea's hand closed over the crystal she wore on a gold chain around her neck, the stone Circe had given her and taught her to use to see into time, to focus and control the present. Now as she looked at the bulls, she saw them for what they were: made of iron—the black metal—and steam-driven, propelled by firing reservoirs of the foul-smelling oil and naphtha that gathered in great pools in the southern wastelands. She saw their creator, a mechanical genius born out of his time in a city far to the northeast—one of Asterodeia's people. His city and civilization had fallen to a barbaric conqueror five hundred years before and would remain forgotten for three thousand years to come. The bulls themselves—created not as supernatural things but to serve as they would be serving now, to pull a plow or wagon without tiring—would disappear into red dust. All memory of them would be reduced to myth. And Aeetes? He had no idea where they came from or what they truly were; it served his purpose to claim, as other rulers had before, that the bulls were the creation of a god.

As Jason approached the first bull, Medea shifted the focus of her concentration. Airflow to the firing chambers diminished; the bull slowed, and the second one pulled even. Both stopped. The crowd breathed "Ahhhh!" The bulls stood with their great heads lowered, white steam rising from their nostrils, seemingly waiting for Jason's command.

That he was no farmer was plain from the awkward way he handled the yoke and the time it took him to hitch the plow. But then no lone man had ever had to yoke oxen so large or with such horns, or use brass chains instead of rope. No sooner was the plow in place than the bulls snorted smoke and lurched ahead. Jason hastily caught the plow handle. The metal blade cut deep into the sod, and he hung on to make a dark line across the green field.

Much to Aeetes' ire, the crowd cheered wildly.

It was Medea who controlled the bulls, who slowed their speed to Jason's, who forced them to turn at the end of each furrow—and made the skill appear to be his. He had held on to the plow and simply stared in amazement the first time the team began a curious side-step and, with a ratchet noise quite unlike any sound he had ever heard, turned as if of their own volition. The first few furrows were shallow and uneven, but gradually he improved at the unfamiliar task.

Aeetes watched impassively, ignoring the cheers of encouragement to Jason from his grandsons and scattered members of the crowd. He did glance toward the river after raucous outcries from the men confined aboard the *Argo.*

"He's going to do it, Father!" Apsyrtus's voice squeaked with indignant excitement. "He's going to take our Fleece!"

The look Aeetes gave his son kept the boy still for an hour.

By midmorning, a quarter of the field had been plowed. For the watchers the novelty of the bulls and barbarian was waning. The noise, smoke, and smell of the creatures was offensive, and as one woman remarked, "Plowing is plowing regardless how it's done." By noon, most of the crowd had drifted away. Birds hopped across the furrows, feeding on the worms and grubs in the virgin soil. Dogs chased field mice dispossessed from ancestral burrows.

Medea sat motionless, gripping the stone at her throat. The sun grew hot on her head, and beads of sweat ran down her face. A blue wasp landed on her arm, fanned its wings, and flew off again. When a servant brought a tray of fruit and wine, she ignored the refreshment as she ignored her discomfort. No one remarked on her odd behavior; she was no more intense than her father.

But the source of Aeetes' intensity was different; where hers was concentration, his was rage. This upstart, this adventurer, was turning his bulls into nothing more than laboring oxen, making their magic worthless, making Aeetes look a fool. There were families here in Aea, even after all these years, who still resented him, who considered him a parvenu, the poor barbarian who had had the good fortune to wed their queen. With Asterodeia gone, they gave him the respect he demanded only because of the merciless discipline and loyalty of his army. The old families would be glad to see him humiliated and to see the barbarian religious relic gone from their ancient shrine.

When Toas came with men to raise a canopy and shield the royal party from the afternoon sun, Aeetes cursed him for not doing so sooner, forgetting that he himself had joked to Toas only the night before that the only shade for which the servants must prepare would be Jason's—and they could control his ghost by a fitting funeral feast and games and sending the *Argo* on its way.

By late afternoon, when it was clear that Jason would complete the plowing, the townspeople returned to watch. Following his team almost at a run, Jason turned over the final furrow and let go of the plow. The bulls turned and headed back to their stable, the muddy plow dragging behind them, bouncing heavily on its side over the field's ribbed surface.

The crowd cheered as Jason went to pick up his shield and weapons to prepare for the other half of his challenge. He'd lost one sandal, and his feet were caked with mud. He was so covered with soot and dust that his teeth appeared snow white. Sweat had traced lines through his grime and plastered his blond hair to his skull, but his eyes glittered gaily as he looked up at Medea and laughed.

"Your bulls are meant for farmers, King Aeetes," he called, "not for a prince. Not for a hero. Without the serpent's teeth, today would be little real challenge."

The king was in no mood to be goaded. He stared morosely at what had been his training field. With the sod destroyed, the place would be a mud slick after every rain for the next ten years. He watched the bulls clanking up the ramp into their stable. Almost out of fuel, they moved as if exhausted. To him the evening air smelled not of their exhaust but of his humiliation.

"You haven't won yet," he said, barely glancing at Jason. "The fruit of the serpent's teeth will defend the Sacred Fleece."

"That serpent, if you remember, mighty Aeetes, had grown old and fat. He was no match for a hero," Jason reminded him. "Or I wouldn't have a portion of his teeth, would I?"

The thinly veiled insult provoked smiles. Aeetes twisted on his bench to see who was amused, taking some time to survey the crowd.

"You're resting, Greek. Resting wasn't part of the bargain." Since his father seemed preoccupied, Apsyrtus decided to speak up. "I was at the feast. I heard what you agreed to do. You promised my father that you'd do exactly as he said."

For the first time, Jason seemed aware of a face other than Medea's and the king's. His too-bright eyes focused on the boy and glinted with malice. His smile faded to scorn, and for a moment it seemed to Medea that two jealous children glared at each other, each resenting the attention the other was getting.

"You are wrong, boy," said Jason. "I accepted your father's challenge, not his domination."

With that, he turned and strode across the field to an oak grove on the other side. He removed a small pouch from a cord tied about his waist and emptied the contents into his hand before scattering what looked like white pebbles onto the plowed ground.

"What will grow up there, Father?" Apsyrtus asked in a whisper.

"Wraiths of warriors killed by the serpent who once guarded the original Spring of Ares."

"And how did this Jason get the teeth?"

"His great goddess gave them to him—or so he claims."

"But if he's under her protection—" the boy began to say, but was silenced by his father and a murmur from the crowd.

A mist was rising up from the field, and in the mist, forms moved. Smokelike, they drifted up from the furrows and billowed into beings, fearsome warriors, their bodies faintly blue with swamp light and decay. They were tall and naked and armed with hide shields and brutal wooden swords serrated with sharks' teeth. Their long black hair was tied back beneath helmets made of animal skulls, some with antlers still attached. When fully formed, they swayed, as though awakened from a long sleep, and then, one by one, moved toward the man who dared to waken them. Soon Jason could be seen only by the blue light glimmering off his shield.

Those who watched felt fear envelop them with the

mist and grew so weak with terror that they could not move to run away. They heard Jason's battle cry but could no longer see him. They saw his sword flash in the mist and heard him pound his shield. Then sword struck sword and battle began, though who fought whom no one could say.

There were no more battle cries, no human sounds, only grunts and gutturals and the thud and crack of metal on hide. Not until light faded from the snow on the mountains and the glacier's icy glare turned pale blue did the sounds of fighting die away. Then Jason appeared, slowly walking out of the mist, wiping his sword with a handful of grass. As he walked, a wind came and blew the mist away, to reveal dark forms lying on the ground. No sooner could they be clearly seen than they began to dissolve back to glowing bones and teeth, back beneath the earth from which they'd been summoned. In the dusk, the scent of death lingered, sickly sweet, and then that too blew away.

Medea was most proud of that last detail, the scent that made the horror real, that served as a fixative to keep the image of a hero in their minds.

SIX

A GREAT SHOUT WENT UP from the Argonauts when they saw Jason was still alive. Their wild voices seemed to release the people of Aea from their miasma of terror. They too began to cheer, as much from relief as admiration. The four brothers ran to Jason, lifted him up on their shoulders and, trailed by friends, carried him before the king.

"Where's my Fleece, mighty Aeetes? Where are the bones of Phrixus?"

The crowd quieted to hear the king's answer. Aeetes regarded Jason in silence. Minutes passed. The king's gaze never wavered, nor did his expression alter—he looked on Jason with pure disgust.

"Give him the Fleece!" shouted a voice in the crowd.

"He won it fairly!" called another. There were mutterings of agreement.

Finally the king leaned over to Medea and whispered, "Do you think the gods helped him?" When she shook her head no, he grunted in agreement, then slowly hoisted himself to his feet, stiff and tired from sitting.

"A party of your men may retrieve the bones of Phrixus from the hide in our tallest beech tree. At any time. My chamberlain will direct you. As for the Sacred Fleece—the priests at the shrine must perform certain rituals. Until those are completed, the Fleece cannot be touched." Aeetes paused to massage a kink in one elbow before continuing. "And to honor you for your valor today, Jason, son of Aeson, heir to the Iolcan throne—and to celebrate the success of your voyage— you and all your companions will feast at the Dawn Palace tonight. As my guests, you will, of course, carry no weapons."

Either as an insult or by force of habit, he waved his hand in dismissal of the suppliant, turned, and made his way to the platform's edge. Preoccupied with negotiating the three steps, much of his downward view being obscured by his stomach, he waited to gain the grass before looking again at the young man. "There will be no long delay," he said. "I promise you, you won't leave here without the Sacred Fleece."

Jason saluted mockingly, and Medea watched him being borne away in triumph toward the *Argo,* saw him acknowledging the praise of her people. Nothing in his manner suggested that anything other than his own strength and will was responsible for his success. She was pleased to see he was so fine an actor.

"I told you he'd take our Fleece!" Apsyrtus shoved past her and down the steps to join his father. "What good will that shrine be without the Fleece of the Sacred Ram?" The boy's sibilant whisper carried well enough for those nearby to hear and would have carried further but for the squeak of axles in the evening air. Chariots and carts were being brought up to carry home the royal household and the nobles. "No one will make sacrifices there now, Father. The priests will starve—"

"Escort your mother and Chalciope back to the palace," Aeetes ordered him, and told his guard and driver: "The princess Medea and I will be alone." He motioned for her to step into the waiting chariot while the two men helped to hoist him up. As he took the reins a cry went up to "Make way for the king!" as they drove through the departing crowd and across the darkening field.

Holding on against the bounce and lurch of the chariot wheels over the sod tufts, Medea stared at the horses' gleaming rumps and wondered how best to manage leaving with Jason. If she went aboard the *Argo* too early, she might be missed at home. Without knowing them, she had no idea how his companions would react to the idea of endangering themselves by taking her along. They might not want her aboard. There was no question of taking any of her servants, not even Lukka. Jason had made it clear that there was no room for servants on such a small ship.

The chariot jolted up onto the palace road, and the wheels whirred over the gravel surface. People walking home stepped aside to avoid being run down.

"Will you give them the Fleece in the morning?" she called over the noise of the chariot wheels.

"No." A flick of the whip, and the horses left the road again to run on the quiet grass. Aeetes leaned closer. "He will be dead by morning. Him and all his friends. And the ashes of the *Argo* will be halfway down to the sea."

She knew him too well to betray her feelings, to protest this shameless reneging on his promises. She wasn't even surprised. "Do you think it's wise to kill them? You gave your word in front of—"

"Wise? In years to come, they'll sing hymns to my wisdom, Medea. You can't believe his story of coming here on a sacred quest. One man might be that naïve, but not fifty. Scoundrels always claim patriotism and piety as their license to steal. These Greeks don't care about the Fleece; they want the trade wealth of Colchis. They don't want poor Phrixus's bones. They want gold. No!" His crown jangled with irate denial. "We'll give the hero and his friends drugged wine—you see to the details for me—and when they're unconscious, the bows of my archers on the roof will sing the ending to their odyssey."

A bonfire burned on the riverbank where the *Argo* was tied up. The crew was celebrating. Wineskins were being passed around with much loud talking and laughter. Most of the laughter mocked Aeetes' warriors, who stood guard between the Argonauts and the city proper. Calciope's sons were there with some of their friends. Several Greeks were bathing; others were trimming a companion's hair or beard or helping one another to dress for the feast. To Medea's surprise, two of the bathers were women, one of them quite beautiful, with long, golden hair that shone like a helmet in the firelight. Both had bodies as wiry and fit as any of the men's.

[*79*]

She tied the horses in a willow thicket and stood watching, waiting for a time when she could call Jason to her without attracting the guards' attention. Long minutes passed, the mosquitoes found her, and Jason showed no signs of leaving his circle of admirers. And so she willed him to come to her.

Come north along the riverbank. Come where there is no firelight, her mind sang to his. Come to the slough where willows bend. Come to me. Come.

He came, looking puzzled but still talking and looking back at his companions, who assumed he was going into the bushes to relieve himself and called ribald suggestions. He didn't see her or the horses until she spoke his name, and then he jumped as if terrified.

"Shh!" She caught hold of his hand to calm him, to draw him near and erase his suspicion of why he'd come here against his will. His hand was dry and rough with calluses, and he smelled of the bulls' exhaust and sour wine. "Listen. We have little time." In whispers she told him of the king's plan and of her own. He listened and agreed. He wasted no time bemoaning Aeetes' perfidy and expressed no surprise at betrayal. It was as if he'd expected as much.

When he took her kidskin bag, he nearly dropped it, surprised by its weight. She watched him walk over to the *Argo* and carelessly toss the bag onto a pile of rope and sail on the deck. The contents clattered so loudly that she winced.

"Where's my share of that wine?" Jason called. "Iphitus, don't be greedy. Bring some to me and Atalanta."

One by one, five of them joined her in the thicket,

whispering their names: Iphitus, Meleager, Argus, Atalanta, and finally Jason. She waited impatiently until they were all mounted and she could lead them away, behind the line of guards, toward the Shrine of Ares some six miles to the south.

The ride was uneventful, yet for the rest of time Medea would remember that evening; the scent of lemon blossoms mingled with woodsmoke would bring an image as fresh and clear as the stars were above the mountains that night. From high overhead came the calls of migrating birds. Twice she heard a hawk cry, or thought she did. The moon was in her crescent phase.

She led them past the city, through orchards and vineyards, avoiding the roads and pathways. Jason rode beside her, close enough to touch her, but he did not. When she reached out to catch his free hand and hold it, as lovers do when riding, he did not see her gesture. Disappointed, she let her hand fall to rest on her bare knee and hoped no one else had noticed. He seemed preoccupied, perhaps nervous. Several times she caught him watching her, but before she could smile he quickly looked away. He was probably shy in front of other people, she told herself.

His companions followed in a single line. She could have been alone, for all the sense of company they gave her, the outsider. They talked softly among themselves. Once she heard Iphitus grumble that they were "foolish to trust her, a barbarian, the daughter of a betrayer who betrays her own father."

The woman warrior, Atalanta, answered: "Some fathers earn betrayal. Mine did. Beware. She speaks our tongue as well as her own—and you must remember what her nephews said of her great powers."

It was the first time she ever heard the term *barbarian* applied to herself—and this from a shaggy-haired man wearing only an apron and blue beads to match the blue paint above his eyes.

"Tell your friends to keep their voices down," she warned Jason, hurt as well as angry. "We don't want guard dogs barking. Or watchmen coming out to see why there are riders in the night." With that, she kicked her horse and galloped ahead into the dark, forcing them to peer after her and ride harder to keep from getting lost.

The shrine stood on a hilltop in a grove of sacred oaks. Its spring sent a creek tumbling down through the woods, gurgling over boulders in its path. There was a cave where the priests who served the god lived—miserably, some said. But then few people had ever been inside the cave for fear of the dragon. The path up to the shrine was narrow and rutted by rain. They left the horses in a ravine. In spite of the darkness and rough footing, the Greeks were remarkably quiet as they climbed the hill. From the dense azalea foliage that rimmed the clearing, they had their first view of the Sacred Fleece.

An apron of white flowstone in front of the cave was lit by the fire burning before the altar. The firelight shone on blood and grease stains where tributes to the god were sacrificed. No priests were in sight.

To the right of the cave was an ancient cypress, its trunk incredibly twisted. The anchoring roots formed gnarled buttresses and thrust thick fingers down into the rocks, cracking the stone as they grew. The Sacred

Fleece hung from the lowest branch of this cypress, the gold-encased horns, the strip of gold fringe that remained, and the gold dust on the curly wool gleaming dully.

Medea pointed to the fleece, but Jason was staring, wide-eyed, in the opposite direction, as were his companions. She looked to see what bothered them and saw the dragon waiting in the gloom.

The dragon stretched out of the shadows, as if its body embraced the hilltop, its great head resting on the edge of the stone apron. Cinder brown with burning purple eyes, it looked as old and evil as it was said to be. A red glow came from deep within its nostrils and half-open jaws. Steam and foul smoke curled out between soot-blackened teeth. One leg was visible, massive and stubby, ending in a foot with three claws like cruel knives.

"Don't be afraid," she was about to say, amused that these heroes should be so gullible, when it occurred to her that fear might teach them to respect her and value what she was giving them.

"They say it was born of the blood of Typhon when Zeus slew that monster." Jason breathed his myth into her ear, his mouth so close that the words tickled and she shivered with pleasure. "How can *you* hope to enchant the offspring of a creature whom only a god dared battle?"

She forced herself to step away. "Because I am Medea. If you doubt me, Prince Jason, then I'll leave you now, before I risk any more for you. The Sacred Fleece means nothing to me, and I have no quarrel with dragons."

She was halfway to the horses before he could catch

up with her. "Please!" He caught hold of her hand, and she felt her knees go weak with wanting him. By sheer willpower she freed herself.

"When the dragon's eyes dim, be ready to take the Fleece," she said, and with that, slipped away into the safety of the night.

She had been here once before, with Circe, as part of her education. Memory of that visit guided her now as she followed the sound and smell of the stream up the hill, feeling her way past dry branches that might snap and betray her. The forest was still; if the priests were ignorant of the presence of strangers on the hill, the wildlife was not. Circling around, she came up on the right side of the dragon's head and stopped there to listen.

This hill was the remnant of a small volcano, Circe had told her, and molten stone, cooling, had formed the hollow tube coiling around the flank. Earth's First Children had seen the rock formation as a stone serpent; some of them had refined the coiling shape into a dragon, which became the guardian of the shrine built in the cave beside it. Over the ages the place had been sacred to a dozen different gods.

Under the dragon's neck was a narrow passage into the cave. The passage walls were worn smooth by the hands of priests feeling their way through the tunnel, as Medea did now. She groped blindly until her fingers found and pulled back the worn hide that screened the opening into the head. Lamps burned behind the amethyst crystal eyes. A fire under a cauldron of water provided smoke and steam. Condensation dripping from the roof into the fire created a constant hissing.

The chamber was as steamy as a laundry but smelled much worse. Gnawed bones and empty wineskins told her the priests often dined in here—for the warmth, probably—which explained the dragon's reputation for mumbling on those rare occasions when it chose to speak.

Her magic was as simple as the priests'; edging her way around the fire, she blew out the eye lamps, and, using a horn ladle leaning against the wall, dashed water over the charring rawhide strips that caused the noxious smoke, soaking them, then pulled back the wind drape so that the smoke and steam could escape through the mouth.

To those waiting and watching outside, the dragon appeared to close its eyes, sigh with a last gust of smoking breath, and settle into sleep.

Outside again, she peered over the dragon's jowl. Argus and Meleager were boosting Jason up to grasp the lowest tree limb. Atalanta stood guard, while Iphitus waited under the branch to catch the Fleece as it fell. She smiled to see them still casting nervous glances over their shoulders, as if the dragon might waken. When Jason had reached the branch and walked out and sat astride it to untie the ropes securing the Fleece, she started back to the horses.

She was halfway there when shouts broke out above. As she stopped to listen, a noisy creature came bounding down the hill in long leaps, breaking branches in its panic to get away. A deer, she thought, but couldn't be sure, and for the first time felt uneasy. Had the Greeks carelessly allowed a priest to escape?

Reaching the horses, she removed their hobbles and

led them to the end of the path, mounted, and sat waiting. Brush rattled. Branches snapped. Bare feet slid on gravel. She heard them coming long before she could see them. They were making no attempt at stealth but running headlong down the path, calling to one another in harsh, excited whispers as to where the horses might be.

"Here."

No sooner had she spoken than they were around her, mounting up. Jason moved awkwardly; he carried the bulky fleece rolled under his arm. "We had to kill a priest," he said by way of greeting. "Another's up there dying. One got away."

"He was young, fast, and frightened," said Atalanta.

Not waiting to hear more, Medea gave her horse a kick and raced off. The priest had less than a mile to run before reaching a noble's villa, where there were horses, hunting dogs, and armed men. The noble would send messengers to warn not only Aeetes but his neighbors, too. Safety lay in reaching the *Argo* as soon as possible, in riding where the horses could run full out without fear of breaking a leg.

She led them down the ravine and across a pasture to an ancient ox road that stretched from Aea south to the dry lands by the inland sea. Along some parts of the road centuries of traffic had worn down the tracks five to ten feet below the level of the bordering land, as a river wears down its bed. Trees grew along the banks, and in warm weather the shade cooled the slow-moving oxen and their drivers. Fronds of sweet fern reached out from the sloping walls, brushing the horses as they passed. The sunken road had one great virtue not lost on Medea; its greenery and high walls would muffle the sound of galloping horses and often completely hide them from view.

A bath for King Aeetes was not a casual event. All but his body slaves were sent away. Reed mats were laid on the bathroom floor and on the floor of the deep tub to keep the royal feet from slipping. When the tub was half full of warm water sweet with bath oils, he was helped in; the water level rose almost to overflowing. Once in and comfortable with a headrest, he liked to be left alone to soak and quietly meditate, free of some of his weight, his crown, and the pain in his overburdened legs. Those who dared to interrupt the peace of Aeetes' bath risked being flogged or worse.

There were three interruptions that night.

The head groom came to report six horses had been stolen from the royal stables, taken out by a rear door always kept barred from inside. And the watchdogs hadn't barked.

The captain of his Corinthian guard came in to say that Jason wasn't with the rest of the Argonauts around the fire and he believed, though he was not sure, that several other Greeks were missing as well.

While the groom and captain were still prostrate on the floor, Chalciope entered. "Have you seen Medea? Her maids say she didn't return from the Field of Ares, but I saw her leave with you. Do you know—"

"She's taking care of something for me," Aeetes said, thinking she was off somewhere mixing up a special drug for that night's wine. But after Chalciope left, he lay back in his tub and stared at the flame of the lamp hanging overhead, remembering Medea's rapt absorption in the day's events. And the way Jason had smiled at her.

"Were any of the guard dogs killed?" he asked the head groom, who remained prostrate on the floor at the top of the bathroom steps. "Were their throats slit to prevent their barking?"

The poor groom, expecting at least death for losing such valuable horses, could hardly speak for fear. Nothing like this had ever happened in his twenty years of service. "N-n-n-no, mighty king."

"The dogs are healthy?"

"Yes," the groom muttered to the floor.

That meant the dogs had not only recognized the thief but were lulled to silence by him. Aeetes himself had chosen those dogs. They were as large and vicious as any ever bred and so hated men that the kennel slaves had to feed them by throwing the meat to them, not daring to approach. The only person he'd ever seen who could pet them was Medea—who claimed it was cruel to keep them chained all their lives. Medea, the only human he had ever completely trusted.

The king moaned softly, as if in pain, and to those who looked at him, it seemed that he suddenly paled and became somehow less than the presence he had been a moment before. His right hand jerked spasmodically, his palm repeatedly slapping the water until a wavelet splashed from under the linen towel draped across the tub and the sweet smell of wet rush was added to the room.

"Are you ill, sir?" his body slave asked, concerned.

Aeetes did not reply but continued to stare up at the lamp flame, his golden eyes as tragic as a toad's. When at long last he spoke, he continued to watch the flame.

"Jason has gone to steal the Sacred Fleece," he said softly, as if talking aloud to himself, "to violate my shrine. When he returns, the guards must be waiting for him. Hidden, so that his crew doesn't suspect anything—or escape with the *Argo*. We will kill Jason and everyone who rides with him. No matter who that may be. We will kill the Greeks, all of them, and burn their ship."

SEVEN

Dogs were baying in the distance when Medea saw the torchlights that marked the roof of the Dawn Palace. Her party was within shouting distance of the *Argo*. At Jason's signal, his crew was to board the ship, take their places at the oars and be ready to pull away as soon as the raiding party was aboard. With any sort of good luck, the *Argo* would be in midstream before the king's guards realized what was happening.

As she leaned down to give the neck of her sweating horse an encouraging pat, what felt like a bird's wing brushed across her shoulder, and Iphitus shrieked a death cry such as singers made to end a tragic song. The cry was so well done that for an instant she didn't think it was real and was irked that he would frighten her with such a sound. Then above the hoofbeats a bowstring sang; there was a soft *thud* of impact, and a rider caught his breath in a sharp hiss. Archers! They had ridden into an ambush!

Strung out for several horse lengths, they were riding where the road cut deep into a bank of clay and sand. Hidden by darkness and the scrub oak above were Aeetes' warriors. Glancing back, she saw Atalanta twist in pain and her horse lurch as she struggled for control.

She didn't have to wonder how her father knew so quickly where Jason had gone; in Aeetes' place she would have known, too. What she counted on was that he had not guessed she was involved and that his warriors did not guess. Without hesitation, she kicked her mount and shouted: "I am Princess Medea! How dare you attack me?" She charged up the bank directly toward the hidden bowmen.

Arrows whistled past, one so close it pulled her hair, and then the bow twangs ceased. There was a scramble in the brush and shouts of anger and alarm as the hoofbeats of the other five horses pounded away down the road.

"After them, you fools! Don't let them escape! The king said to kill!"

"But it's the princess Medea!"

"Those are the king's horses!"

"She wouldn't be with the Greeks!"

"Who else would dare to charge us?"

And then more urgently: "Get her horse! Stop that horse!"

She galloped through their midst, pulled the stallion sharply to the left and plunged down the embankment. The horse nickered loudly in fear. She could feel him sliding, and twice he stumbled over tangled vines. She kept her seat only by sheer will. Clinging on, she regained the road as the horse danced and reared. A spear cracked against a boulder and glanced off. The shaft hit the stallion's left haunch and scared him into a run.

Crouching low against his neck, she gripped as hard as she could with her knees. The horse was wheezing with exhaustion and fear, and its sweat burned her cheek. Every sound she heard spoke of disaster: The men behind were shouting; from the west other soldiers answered; from ahead came Iphitus's involuntary screams of pain. As she caught up with Jason, she heard a large company of riders galloping toward them. Hunting dogs bayed behind them.

Failure hadn't occurred to her, or the thought of being wounded or killed. There was no time now for magic, cleverness, or tricks. In the dark an arrow had no respect for learning or lineage. She could cry out for Circe's help, if Circe was near, but Circe might not wish to help a man who had profaned a shrine and killed the priests of a god he professed to worship.

From around the bend galloped horses so white they gleamed in the dark, the mounts of the king's Corinthian guards. Seeing them, she realized that Aeetes had guessed she had led Jason to the shrine. He had sent his Corinthians to kill her so that no one would know she had betrayed him—or would ever dare to say so.

"The river," she called to Jason. "Let the horses swim!" An arrow hissed past her head and thocked into a tree.

The riverbank was less than fifty yards away, but the Corinthians caught up with them before they reached the water. Sword clanged on sword. A wounded horse screamed. The air smelled of blood and horse sweat and fear.

She didn't try to use her dagger; it was all she could

do to ride. When the horse shied away from jumping into the water, she was catapulted off—and the sword blow meant for her severed the animal's spine. The stallion's death scream was the last thing she heard before the shock of hitting the cold water. The impact knocked the wind from her. She went under, flailing wildly, tumbled by the current until her head and shoulder struck against a floating wooden mass.

Someone grabbed her by the hair and pulled, but she had no breath to cry out at the pain. Hard, callused hands gripped her right arm. With bruising roughness, she was hauled out of the water and dropped onto the *Argo*'s deck like a weighty fish. She lay there stunned and coughing, wet hair plastered over her face, vomiting muddy water, gulping precious air. When a man tripped over her and cursed in Greek, she roused herself enough to sit up.

Someone was shouting orders to the oarsmen, who were trying to hold the *Argo* steady against the current. In the water, terrified horses screamed; hooves pounded against the hull. Darkness made it hard to see; the men leaning over the railing, their exposed buttocks white from lack of sun, were the most prominent feature of her view. A soggy bundle smelling of mud and dirty, wet wool sloshed onto the deck—the Sacred Fleece.

After it came Jason, shouting orders even as he was pulled aboard. "There! Beneath the oars! Grab him before he goes down again!"

"The spear went through him! He's pinned to the horse!"

"Break the spear!"

They were almost gentle as they laid Iphitus beside

her. When she smelled the odors escaping from the wound in his gut, she knew it would have been far kinder to let him drown. Already too weak to scream, he moaned in agony. She reached out to feel the pulse in his throat. Water splashed onto her arm, and Atalanta clambered over the rail unaided; panting, she paused to catch her breath and then, without a word or wasted movement, crossed the deck to help in the rescue of Argus and Meleager.

Horns were being sounded. There was a shout, a surge of oars, and the ship moved out into midstream. Medea's last glimpse of Aea was the bonfire on the shore.

The current was with them, and they had a head start. They rowed in shifts, making great speed. But always behind them, from around every bend in the river, came the torchlights and lanterns of their pursuers. Aeetes' lead ship was followed by two more, and three more followed behind those. The Colchian war galleys were smaller and faster than the *Argo,* and their crews knew every inch of the river.

For all the attention the Argonauts paid to Medea, she might have been as lifeless as Jason's other trophy. For a time, she sat where she'd been put, numb with cold and the reality of her decision. Iphitus lay to her left; in front of her, Meleager curled like a sick child. Argus sat slumped against the water barrel and clutched his wounded arm. Atalanta had taken her place at the oars, and Jason was with the helmsman. In the darkness, she could hear him call to the lookout man: "Lynceus, what do you see?"

Each time Lynceus would answer patiently and

calmly. The only time he showed excitement was when the *Argo* scraped a floating tree. Submerged roots struck the hull, dead branches rattled and snapped against the oars. Dry leaves and brittle twigs rained onto the deck.

The outcry wakened Iphitus. He began to twist and moan and claw at his wound, as if trying to tear out the pain. The Argonauts ignored him, but his great agony woke Medea from her own misery. Sitting up, she looked for her leather bag, finally saw its dark shape against the whiteness of the old sails and crawled to it on her hands and knees. From it she took her hooded cape, and when she'd put that on felt better, as if shielded not only from the cold but from indifference. Then, reaching to the bottom of the bag where her precious chest was hidden, she touched the hidden spring of the lid and removed several vials.

Before Iphitus could cry out again, she pressed her fingers hard against the base of his skull, and he went limp. She poured a generous dose of opium syrup into his mouth and tilted his head back. Then, with scraps of sail, she packed the damaged flesh as best she could to keep the air from causing more pain and, with the dressing done, found a fleece to cover him against the damp cold.

Turning then to Argus and Meleager, she gave them pellets of beaver liver, bitter with willow bark. They swallowed the drug, only because they were afraid not to, and let her bind their wounds as best she could in the darkness. Even after she brought them cloaks and covered them, they still feared her. She was a witch; they had seen her enchant a dragon.

When the drugs took full effect and Iphitus had quieted into his last sleep, she leaned against the rail and watched the white wake foam. Her world had suddenly narrowed to this deck and the stars overhead. All she had ever loved was being swiftly left behind. Far in the distance flecks of flame appeared—the lights of Aeetes' ships. If the Argonauts could not escape, she had chosen death.

"Can your magic heal Iphitus?"

She nearly jumped at Jason's question; the noise of the oars had covered his approach. "No. He's mortally wounded."

"Your sister's sons said you can heal all but lepers." He sounded disappointed in her.

"My nephews are wrong."

"Iphitus is the brother of King Eurystheus of Mycenae," he said, as if hoping that would make her try harder.

"I have put him to sleep to ease his pain. That's all I can do. . . ." Her arm brushed Jason's, and she felt a sticky wetness. "You're bleeding!"

"It's just a sword cut." He'd wrapped a dirty leather strip around it.

She bandaged him as she had the others, and while he thanked her, she knew he was disappointed. He had expected instant healing, magic—perhaps the boys had told him she had only to touch a wound and it healed. When she had finished, he walked away without even asking her how she was. She stared after him in the darkness, hurt and angry, thinking that by his manner she might as well be a handmaiden, a servant. Then almost immediately she remembered how tired he must be, and worried, and distracted by responsibility for his men—and she forgave him.

The wind changed; the sail was raised and the *Argo* sped on. From the marshes along the banks, a panther roared. Wolves and jackals barked. Occasionally a sturgeon or other great fish leaped with an alarming splash, frightened by the passage of the ship through night feeding grounds. The wind faded; the sail was lowered again, and some who slept were wakened to resume rowing.

In the hour before dawn, when fog settled over the marshlands and made the night still darker, Medea wrapped her cloak around her and curled up against the pile of worn sailcloth. Aeetes' daughter, who had never slept in less than luxury, slept now on rags and dreamed disturbing dreams.

She woke, suddenly afraid, and saw Phrixus standing beside her, his form and features inexplicably clear in the night. He was looking at the Golden Fleece, which still lay on the deck where Jason had dropped it. He was younger than she remembered him, and far more handsome. He wore a crown of vines and fruit, as if prepared for some ceremony. He turned and looked down at her but gave no sign of recognition. Instead, his gaze slid to Iphitus. Such pity filled his face then that she also looked at the dying man. Iphitus, too, glowed with an unnatural light. As girl and ghost watched, Iphitus stirred; a mist rose from his body and became a separate form, which sat up and looked dazedly about before fixing its gaze on Prince Phrixus. The two beheld one another in some strange form of recognition; Phrixus stretched out a hand and helped Iphitus rise. For seconds they stood there, engaged in some communion only they could share before the light that was their forms went dim and faded.

There was no outcry. No one else appeared to have noticed anything. The rowers kept on rowing; none of the sleepers stirred. Perhaps she was still dreaming? Yet it came as no surprise when she touched Iphitus and found that he was dead.

It was almost dawn. Fog hid Aeetes' ships. In the gray mist, all that could be seen was the water near the ship and a dark band of green along the bank. Between the swamp and the sea was a vast tidal marsh cut through with river channels and dotted by brackish bogs. By first light, the *Argo* slipped in to hide in one of these side channels, a near-tunnel of giant reeds and bamboo.

Any talking now was done in whispers. Oars were lifted. The ship was poled ahead carefully, quietly, deep into the reeds. The anchor stone was let down slowly so that there was no betraying splash. The ship swung on its tether, pushed by languid current, and came to rest against a root mass that squished, spongelike, and gave out a rich odor of mud and rotting vegetation.

Minutes passed. In the reeds the nesting wrens and warblers resumed their predawn songs. Ducks were quacking somewhere nearby. Geese flew over, talking. Medea shivered with cold and nerves while insects whined around her ears.

Suddenly a bittern gave its harsh warning cry; an otter chirred alarm; there were soft splashes as unseen creatures took refuge in the water. The marsh went still again. Only the river and mosquitoes sang.

It gave her a queer feeling to hear her father's ships approach. His men called to one another over the creak and thump of the oars, their voices in the fog as separate and distinct as bird cries, high-pitched with excitement. The dense air made them seem closer than they were. Then, between the reeds, a movement caught her eye. A ship came into view, its image softened and dimmed by the mist. Another followed, then a third, a fifty-oared vessel bearing the royal banner and canopy. There was a wide chair on the royal platform beneath the gold drape. In the chair sat a small figure, nearly hidden by a gold shield shaped like a rayed sun disk.

"Apsyrtus!" She whispered the name in shock.

Aeetes had not come. Aeetes—who hated the sea, who was at best a poor sailor, whose very weight slowed a ship—had sent his only son. Which meant that the Colchians intended to follow the *Argo* as long as necessary and to fight if they had to in order to return Medea and the Sacred Fleece to Colchis.

With that royal shield, Apsyrtus spoke with the power of Aeetes the Mighty; he could demand the aid of every king along the Black Sea coasts. Apsyrtus, who was seven years old, had been granted this honor in his first year of manhood. This boy with none of her mother's blood could not only take her kingdom but might also make her a prisoner, decide if she lived or died, cause her to lose Jason. Anger as cold and pervasive as the fog enveloped her.

Had it been up to her, there and then the *Argo* would have pursued those six ships and one by one rammed them, spilling that ridiculous little boy and his men into the cold current to sink or swim as fate allowed. But it wasn't up to her.

When the enemy ships had passed out of hearing, the *Argo*'s anchor stone was raised. As quietly as she had entered the channel, she was eased back into the mainstream to drift behind Aeetes' ships in the shelter of the fog.

Where the river reached the sea, the Argonauts fled north as the Colchians headed south and west in search of them. Jason thought the ruse a good one. All his men agreed. The Colchians would assume the *Argo* had taken the most direct route home and spend days in aimless pursuit. When they realized their mistake, they would give up and go home. The ease with which they had outwitted their enemies delighted the jubilant Argonauts. A wineskin was passed to toast their cleverness.

Medea didn't share in the celebration, nor did she say she thought it premature. She had no time to talk. When the *Argo* entered the rough water where river and sea current met, the waves buffeting the ship woke the two wounded men and made them moan with pain. She quickly put them to sleep again.

The Argonauts saw only that she cradled each man's head in her hands and their eyes fell shut. Then, from the leather bag they saw her take an obsidian blade sharper than any razor, two copper needles curved like new moons, silk cords and pliant white sinews. With the addition of vials, oil-skin packets and a small wooden tray to hold her tools, she set to work.

Using sail scraps as rags and the cook's kettle for a basin, she washed the wounds with seawater and staunched the bleeding with a magic touch—or so it appeared to her audience. Onto both Argus's arm and Meleager's thigh she dusted a fine gray powder, trimmed and fitted the torn flesh together, and sewed it with sinews and silk. "As neat as if she were making a boot," one man said later. There was some muttering at this, but none dared to openly question her; she had enchanted a dragon.

Absorbed in her work, she paid no attention to her audience. There was a challenge in these repairs, in reattaching muscle to muscle, tendon to tendon, to ensure that the arm or leg would work properly after healing. When ready to bandage, she discarded the sailcloth scraps as too dirty. Folded in her bag was a tunic of Egyptian cotton, soft and fine and durable. She hesitated for a moment—it was her favorite garment—then shrugged, took her knife and cut the thing into neat strips and began to wrap Argus's arm.

Had she deliberately schemed to win Greek approval, she couldn't have been more successful. That costly fabric would have been cherished by their women and saved for special occasions, passed from mother to daughter until it fell apart from years of wear. To see her use a garment so precious to bind wounds touched them as few things could have.

As she started to wrap Meleager's thigh and found the going awkward, three men left their oars to help, but Atalanta got there first. Kneeling beside Medea, she gently lifted the injured leg and held it for as long as was necessary. Neither spoke until Medea began to put away her tools.

"Can you help me?" Atalanta whispered shyly. She lifted her hunting tunic just far enough to reveal a bruised and bloody knot over her lower left rib. A few inches from the lump, a splintered stick protruded, the remains of an arrow shaft.

"You rowed through the night with that in you?"

"I didn't want to die in Colchis."

The simple answer nearly startled laughter from Medea, but she controlled herself. With a grave nod, she motioned for the other to lie down.

Atalanta hesitated. "I'll need wood to bite on; I don't want the men to hear me cry out."

"There'll be no pain."

"You'll enchant me as you did Meleager?"

Medea frowned. Is that what they thought she'd done? All the time she'd spent learning the exact pressure points, and now these Greeks viewed her skill as *magic*? Perhaps it was just as well. "It won't hurt," she said.

Atalanta submitted to treatment with great reluctance, obviously not used to trusting her body to anyone for any reason. When she felt the quick and expert pressure of the fingertips at the base of her skull, she tried to twist away and escape. As her eyes closed, her look was that of an animal that knows it is fatally trapped and has resigned itself.

Working against the roll of the ship over the offshore swells, it was still a fairly simple matter to remove the arrowpoint from the pocket it had made beneath the skin. There was little more to this slim body than muscle, bone, and skin. Stitching up the wound, Medea wondered about Atalanta, so solitary, so self-contained; why had she joined this crew?

By midmorning the fog was gone, and the *Argo* was alone on the sea. There was no sign of habitation along the coast. Always in view of land, they sailed north and west and did not stop until late afternoon.

They came ashore in a cove on an island of tall pines where goats had been seen jumping down over the rocks. The *Argo* was pulled up onto the most sheltered portion of the beach. Lookouts were posted. A fire pit was dug in the sand and lined with stones, wood gathered, the ship's water bags rinsed and refilled at a spring.

With no slaves to serve them, each Argonaut had duties, which he set to do immediately. Ignoring her wound, Atalanta took her bow and spear and went off to hunt, as did two of the men. Others waded into the surf with fishing nets while two scavenged the tide pools, gathering seaweed and shellfish. Argus, obviously feeling better, examined the hull of this ship he had designed and built, then set a bucket of pine pitch on to warm by the fire so that he might repair leaks.

Medea had no chores of her own and was feeling rather left out. She'd been hoping Jason would go walking with her so that they might be alone together, but Jason was as busy as the others and had no time for her. After overseeing Meleager being carried ashore and making him comfortable, she walked alone on the beach for the sheer pleasure of free movement. Sitting for hours on a plank deck crowded with bodies and gear had left her stiff and sore. Her shoulder ached where she had been pulled aboard; she was hungry and dirty, and her head itched from dried river mud.

Some distance from the cove she saw several of the men stacking driftwood in a pile while others were gathering branches, pine cones and lumps of pitch. She watched for a time, looking out across the water at the mainland, listening to these strangers' voices calling to one another, thinking that from here her mountains seemed so distant. Suddenly she wanted Lukka, and her own bathtub, and a fine meal and the perfumed comfort of her own bed. And privacy! Above all, *privacy.*

When she traveled on her own ship, it was in the comfort of a pillowed divan under an awning with side curtains that could be shut tight against inclement weather. But that was as a princess of Colchis, not a runaway. A runaway, she reminded herself sternly, could expect discomfort.

Following a creek up into the cool, piney shade, she found a pool deep enough to swim in, where she bathed and washed her hair. Dressed again, she was combing out the tangles with a hazel twig when she became aware that someone was watching her. Just then Atalanta slipped out from among the trees.

She wore a small chamois like a cape, its slender ankles clasped in one hand, her spear in the other. The chamois' head drooped over her shoulder, its eyes glazed. A drop of blood hung jewel-like from one delicate nostril. More blood had congealed on Atalanta's arm, dark red on golden tan.

"I came to thank you. To tell you I am grateful." She paused, as if wanting to say more but unsure if she should. Medea waited. "How can you do this?" Atalanta burst out. "How can you be so learned and skilled and so much a fool at the same time? To trust *Jason!* To trust any man? To risk your life and knowledge? Risk the anger of your goddess? Risk desertion—"

"He won't betray me! He loves me! He's sworn a sacred oath never to betray me!" The very suggestion made Medea angry.

"So he's told us," came the quiet response. "Several times. But before you believe a man's sacred oath, you should know his motives and his true gods. You should know what he hopes to gain by swearing—what bargain he is making."

"Why are you with him if you don't trust him? Why is he your captain?"

"Because Hercules refused to be. All the men wanted Hercules to lead us, but the omens favored Jason and Hercules refused to go against the omens. I wouldn't have trusted Hercules either, but then I trust no man." Atalanta shifted the weight of the chamois. "I have cause not to. My father is Iasus, king of Arcadia. When my mother, Clymene, gave birth to me, my father was bitterly disappointed—he wanted a son. He had me taken to the nearest hill and exposed, to die. It was a cold spring night. Wolves were howling—"

"Your mother didn't stop him?"

Atalanta never smiled, but she nearly did so now at this naïveté. "Women may have power in Colchis, but not in Arcadia. Even if she had wanted me . . ." A shrug, and the story went on. "A she-bear saved me, or so I'm told. A mother bear who had lost her cub and so made do with me. Her milk kept me alive. Her long fur kept me warm. A tribe of hunters found me with her. Because the she-bear is sacred to Artemis, the hunters knew I was under her protection. They took me to their camp and raised me in honor, training me as a hunter, like my goddess. To honor Artemis and myself, I have become the best. Like her, I am brave and chaste, and will remain so."

"Does your father know you survived?"

"Yes. He still refuses to recognize me." She kicked a willow root with such violence that Medea jumped. "Never trust a man!"

"But men saved your life."

"Artemis saved my life! She chose the men to help me. To refuse would have brought her wrath on them, and for the rest of their lives they would have come back empty-handed from the hunt—if they returned at all. Survival, not virtue, motivated their decision to help me."

With that, she turned and left, leaping down from rock to rock as if she had inherited the same grace as the chamois she carried so easily. Medea stared after her, disturbed. The daughter of a king exposed to die? Jason had been taken to a hilltop to be given to the horse tribes. Was infanticide a habit with these Greeks, a custom of "home" her father never bothered to mention? Or were even their kings so poor that they couldn't feed their children? As for Atalanta's warning about Jason—she was plainly wrong. Jason had sworn his love; she had felt it in his touch, his kiss. Still, Atalanta had known him far longer.

A cloud of midges as black and erratic as her thoughts descended on her, and she escaped both by running. Before she was halfway back to camp, she could smell the meat roasting over the fire, reminding her that she'd eaten little for the past two days. Two days? It seemed like a year.

She would remember that first meal of the voyage as one of the best she had even eaten: kid seasoned with seasalt and roasted over the driftwood fire, fresh oysters from the cove, seaweed that added its own exotic flavor when wrapped around a shred of meat, bread stolen from the ovens of Aea and now toasted on green sticks. Her spirits rose with each bite.

Jason sat beside her, giving her his complete attention, and the most tender bits of meat. He introduced her to all of his companions—there had been no time to do so before—and she learned they represented every court in Greece.

By his account and their own, few of the Argonauts were ordinary mortals. Idmon said he was Apollo's son; Caeneus, king of the Lapiths, had once been a woman who had asked the gods to make her a man and, he said, the request had been granted. Pollux was the son of Zeus and Leda, while Calais and Zetes claimed to be the sons of the North Wind. Butes was a beemaster, and Mopsus spoke the language of birds. Jason himself, he confided to Medea, was under the protection of the goddess Hera, and Athena spoke to him through the oaken beam of the *Argo*.

As Jason talked on, it became clear to her that he was speaking of the Great Goddess, merely called by other names in his land, but when she suggested this, he vehemently denied it, as if he found the idea insulting. She didn't pursue the topic, not wanting the smallest disagreement to spoil her pleasure in his company. She kept looking at him, admiring the curly ringlets of his beard, how his eyes changed from green to yellow when he faced the light, the fine line of his nose, the perfection of his mouth, the way his hands seemed aware of the texture of everything he touched—especially her arms.

"Three of our company left us in Mysia," Jason told her after a considerable amount of wine. "One was Hercules. If he had come along to meet Aeetes, this would have been a different story. But he had other loyalties."

Although Jason spoke softly, she noted that those seated nearby turned to look at him, their expressions less than friendly. He fell silent, distracted by an ash on his wrist. Orpheus chose that moment to begin playing his lyre, and everyone stopped talking to listen. It was as if he wanted to change the subject, Medea thought, but did not understand why that should be. Hercules was unknown to her.

"I will sing the praises of Iphitus," said Orpheus. "Those who wish to may join the song."

The great stack of driftwood she'd watched the men collecting became a pyre for the dead prince of Mycenae. Torched at sunset, the dry wood crackled into flame and, with the pitch-soaked pine, soon was blazing hot. Black smoke billowed into the twilight sky. If anyone was watching, Medea thought, both fire and smoke made a beacon visible for miles. Better to have given the body to the sea or left it in the swamp for the carrion birds.

That night, wrapped in a warm fleece as well as her cloak, she slept dreamlessly, exhausted, only to be wakened at dawn by the cry of the lookout from high in a pine.

"Sails! Three sails! To the southeast!"

By the time the *Argo* was loaded and launched, three more sails had appeared.

EIGHT

THE COLCHIAN FLEET FOLLOWED THEM day and night, allowing neither rest nor escape. The wind died away to a breeze and the weather turned unseasonably warm. The Argonauts had to row in shifts and could seldom risk landing for fresh water. Fish grilled on the ship's charcoal brazier became their only food; when the charcoal was gone, they ate the fish raw.

To Medea's surprise and irritation, the Argonauts appeared to be enjoying all this, as if deprivation and exhaustion were no more than a game. The raw fish didn't bother them, or the stinking water. They cheered when the pursuing sails grew small in the distance and yelled insults when the Colchian ships drew closer. "We've been in worse danger," Jason assured her, amused by her worry. "We always escape. My goddess watches over me."

Near the mouth of the vast river that served as the main trade route to Hyperborea, the fine weather ended in a storm with sheeting rain and hail. Seeking shelter in the lee of what Jason took to be an island, the Argonauts instead found themselves behind the tip of a narrow cape. They were trying to come about when a wind gust pushed the *Argo* on her side; only the sail's collapse kept them from capsizing. Oars snapped. Men were thrown overboard and had to be rescued. In the downpour, the Colchians entered the channel behind them and cut off their escape. The smaller ships came as close as possible in the choppy sea and surrounded the *Argo*. The Colchian bowmen took up their positions for attack, waiting only for the waves to subside.

While his companions struggled with the damaged ship, Jason came to where Medea sat pulling deck splinters from her knee. She had fallen when the boat tipped. "You must trust me now," he said, pulling her to her feet. "Trust me, and remember that I adore you, no matter what happens."

With that, he put his arm around her, but what she assumed was going to be a reassuring embrace was not. His grip tightened, and he spun her around to face the king's ship. Pulling her against him as a living shield, he held his sword to her throat. "Look frightened!" he ordered, then shouted to her kinsmen. "If you want the Princess Medea to live, you will lay down your weapons and bargain with me!"

"And if we don't?"

"Your prince will lose all he was sent to recover. Most of you will die—or wish you had. We are the favorites of the gods! If you attack us, you will fail. For all of time to come, the sons of men will remember only your humiliation. Songs will be sung of the failure of Prince Apsyrtus, son of Aeetes the Mighty."

There was no immediate response. Through the

streaking rain, officers could be seen talking with the prince, sheltered under his golden canopy. The ships bobbed on the waves. The Colchian archers stood waiting for the signal to attack. Other men were tying grappling hooks to ropes, ready to pull the *Argo* close and secure her for boarding.

With his beard brushing her cheek each time she moved, Medea tried to take comfort from Jason's embrace, but found that difficult. She *was* serving as his shield.

"You're outnumbered five to one," the Colchian admiral shouted. "Your ship is damaged. You're in no position to bargain. You can't escape. All we ask is that you return Princess Medea and the Sacred Fleece. If you do, we'll let you leave our sea unharmed."

Jason pretended to discuss this with the Argonauts, but what he said to them was: "On my signal, be ready to row faster than you've ever rowed before. Watch for an opening between their ships." He allowed several minutes to pass before answering the enemy. "My companions feel your argument has merit. But there is the matter of honor to consider. Where the Fleece is concerned, I took only what I had earned. If Prince Apsyrtus wants the honor of taking home his sister and the Fleece, let him also earn that. Let him be man enough to claim them from my hand, on my ship. Although his father broke his promise to me, I swear no harm will come to the prince from any of the *Argo*'s crew. He shall be given all the respect the son of King Aeetes deserves."

Through the wind and rain came the high voice of a willful boy arguing with his elders and a man's shout of: "Don't be taken in by Greek lies! Can't you see he wants you as a hostage so he can bargain his way out?"

That's true, Medea thought, watching Apsyrtus rise and lean the golden shield of power against his chair so that he could tie on his sword belt. As his admiral reached out to touch his arm, as a man would touch his son in a plea for common sense, Apsyrtus threatened him with that sword. The admiral stepped back, surprised, then, with obvious reluctance, bowed to the royal will.

"Do you agree to a state of truce?" the Colchian called to Jason.

"We do."

As the king's ship moved closer, Jason warned his companions: "Get ready. We'll move out soon."

"Are you going to take him hostage?" she asked.

"No," Jason assured her, "I wouldn't do that."

The *Argo* shuddered as the other ship bumped against her side. Lynceus leaned over the railing to help the boy aboard.

Prince Apsyrtus stepped onto the *Argo*'s deck with more confidence than most men would have shown in this situation. After pausing for a brief look at the crudely carved ram's head on the bow, he calmly brushed salt water from the side flaps of his leather skirt, then adjusted his cape. Once satisfied with his costume, he surveyed the crew, one by one, until his glance fell on the Fleece, nailed to the mast. The gold dust matted in the wool shone in the rain; the glass eyes looked quite dead. Ignoring Jason as completely beneath his notice, the prince fixed his half sister with a look of contempt. "Since you helped these filthy barbarians steal the Sacred Fleece," he said, "you can take it down and carry it back to my ship for me."

The trio stood for a moment in silence, Jason still holding Medea, his blade still at her neck. The boy's glance flicked over him, dismissing him. He turned on his heel. "Bring the Fleece, Medea," Apsyrtus ordered. "Now!"

"Now!" With a shout of rage, Jason threw Medea sprawling on the deck. As she fell, she saw the shining arc of his sword come down in a vicious sweep and heard the blade crack against and through Apsyrtus's back. The boy was knocked against the rail by the blow, almost cut in half. The great bronze sword arced again, and again, the tip thudding into the wooden deck like an axe into a butcher's block, and as he hacked away, Jason shouted "Now! Now! Now!" in a chant of murderous triumph. Like a cook gone berserk, she thought in horror.

The *Argo* lunged ahead, bumping aside the encircling ships, pushing past. There were outraged shouts from the Colchians, and arrows flew, finding no target. Perhaps the bowmen were in shock, or feared to kill her, Medea thought, or—more likely—feared to overshoot the *Argo* and hit their own men in the ship opposite. On the king's ship, a eunuch screamed—the boy's personal body slave.

As the *Argo* slid out of the encircling ring, Jason stooped and grabbed pieces of the body and flung them overboard, shouting, "Take this to Aeetes! And this! And this! Tell him this is how Jason honors liars!"

Still clutching his sword, he dropped to his hands and knees, to duck the arrows, she thought, then saw him lick up some of Apsyrtus's blood and spit it out again. He did this three times before he raised his head, and their eyes met. Her eyes were wide with puzzled horror, his with revenge. Blood dripped from his face and beard. Blood covered his hands and arms. Individual drops of blood were congealing in his wet blond hair.

"To keep his ghost from haunting me—that's what I must do!" he panted. "Spit out his blood to keep his ghost away from me!"

She looked away, wanting to vomit. On the northern horizon a patch of blue showed through the clouds, but all she could see was Apsyrtus's face as his head was thrown overboard. His partial torso had twisted as it fell, and his eyes had stared back into hers. He had looked so surprised, so bewildered—Jason had struck so quickly that there was life still in those eyes. She pulled herself to her knees and looked over the rail to where he'd fallen. The black fins of sharks slid through the water behind the *Argo*.

The Argonauts rowed as fast as they could out of that natural harbor. The Colchians made no attempt to follow; in spite of the sharks the men had begun diving, trying to collect the pieces of Aeetes' only son to take home to him—and doubtless trying to decide how they would break the news of this third and gravest loss. Incoming sharks moved past the *Argo;* eagles and scavenger gulls circled overhead, indifferent to the weather, drawn by the scent of blood.

For the rest of the gray afternoon the only sounds aboard the *Argo* were the creak of oars and brief, necessary exchanges between the men repairing the sail. No one felt like talking. Seemingly no one could look at either Jason or Medea.

After repeating several times, "Aeetes lied to me! He was going to kill us! You all know that!" and getting no response, no verbal absolution of his treachery, Jason had hoisted up buckets of water to wash himself and sluiced the blood from the deck.

Medea watched a school of porpoises appear, whistling and leaping through the waves in joyous celebration of life. Often they would surround a ship and escort it for miles, always a good omen. But this school turned away when still far off and vanished beneath the surface. She thought that only fitting.

She was in shock. She had never liked Apsyrtus and did not truly mourn him, but she did mourn the manner in which he had met death—a prince of the Dawn Palace—and by whose hand. Jason's. Jason had killed him. Beautiful, soft-spoken Jason with his lazy summer eyes had lied and murdered. Only fear of the Greeks' total contempt kept her from screaming aloud.

True, he had said no crew *member* would attack the boy, and none had. The captain had killed him. But that was trickery of the lowest kind; that could not be justified by the fact that Aeetes had broken his word.

The sail was repaired and raised again. A northwest wind pushed the clouds away. The temperature was falling rapidly when the oaken beam of the *Argo* began to creak. She would have dismissed the sounds it made as the protests of wet wood under wave strain but for the reactions of the Argonauts. They stopped rowing and stared at Jason, who had turned deathly pale.

"We have to leave the *Argo,*" he told her anxiously.

"To get food and water?"

"No." He avoided meeting her eyes. "She refuses to carry us—you and me—until we have been purified." Seeing that she still didn't understand, he pointed to the prow. "The goddess spoke. The beam spoke.

Didn't you hear her? She doesn't want us aboard. We are unclean, responsible for death. We endanger the ship this way!"

"But I killed no one," she protested. "You—"

"If you hadn't betrayed Aeetes and helped us take the Fleece, today could never have happened," he said. "Today was the result of your actions."

From the expressions of the others, it was obvious they believed and agreed. Even Atalanta looked uneasy when Medea met her glance.

Medea turned and studied the island-dotted coastline. As far as she could see, there was no trace of human habitation. The hills were dense with deep forest. Yet for all its isolation, the scene looked familiar to her, and she suddenly remembered why. "Circe!" she said aloud. "Her island's there. Just over the horizon. We'll go to her. She will purify us!"

At that, the beam spoke again. Jason turned still more somber. "She approves," he whispered. "The goddess approves of your choice."

NINE

THE BEACH HISSED AND BLEW BUBBLES from tiny holes as
each wave receded. Sandpipers fed along the water's
edge, stabbing slender beaks into the slurry of sand and
foam. The birds ignored Jason, who stood knee-deep
in the shallows, shading his eyes with his hands, watching the *Argo* leave without him. The ship was far beyond the breakers, moving as fast as wind and oars
would push it from Circe's island.

All had agreed that, after their purification, the pair
would meet the ship again at a point six days' walk
down the mainland coast. This would give the Argonauts time to rest and to repair the ship while the
pair who had been purified spent the required isolation
time alone on the journey.

Medea stood on the shore watching as the sun slid
below the last of the clouds and glared across the
water, blinding Jason. With a visible sigh, he turned
and slowly waded to shore. Their life together was
never supposed to be this way, she thought, seeing his

dejection; it was supposed to be light and laughter, love and adventure and comradeship—not betrayal and pursuit, mud, blood and death.

"Do you know the way?" He sounded like he didn't care if she did or not.

"Yes."

She set off, and he fell into step beside her. Neither felt like talking. There was nothing to say. She carried her leather bag, he only his weapons.

Windrows of storm-washed driftwood littered the beach. For long stretches the tangle formed a wall. Here and there, the body of an animal drowned in some river's spring flood was part of the debris. The smell attracted carrion feeders; eagles perched among the roots; vultures fought with gulls and crows and foxes.

Three young lions lay at ease in the branches of a barkless tree and regarded the humans through satiated eyes. Tails twitched as the interlopers passed. One cat sniffed the wind and coughed, but none bothered to get up. Jason, still searching the horizon for his ship, didn't even see them.

When the barrier of beach debris finally permitted it, Medea led them inland. Night was falling. The noise of the surf faded, replaced by forest sounds and the scent of leaf mold. Quiet as it was, she was uneasy. When she'd come here before, it had been Circe's doing. She'd never dared, or even considered, coming here of her own volition. To arrive unannounced, in the company of Jason, to ask a great favor . . .

A bear padded out of a thicket and stopped, surprised to see them, then reared up on its haunches. Its jaws moved oddly, as if it were trying to speak. Jason drew his sword and stepped in front of her.

"If you ever want to leave this island, kill nothing here." She slipped between him and the bear, thus shielding both from harm. "Circe allows no killing here."

"What could she do?" he said defiantly.

"Change your shape to teach you a new perspective. You might become a lion, or a bear, or a pig, depending on what she thinks of you."

He frowned but sheathed his sword and said sarcastically, "Maybe you should protect me. You're the one who charmed the dragon."

"Yes," she said and walked on. Tired and heartsick, uneasy at the idea of meeting Circe with their request, she was at the limit of her patience.

With twilight the forest became an awesome place. Shapes and shadows moved on the fringe of their vision, following them. The grunting of pigs was plain enough, and the barking of deer, but what were those footsteps off to the right, crunching through deep leaves? And that fleshy, inquiring snuffle of a hunting beast that seemed now to be ahead of them, now at their heels? Was some hungry creature stalking them, or was it merely curious? Without warning, a large gray baboon stepped out of the bushes and gripped her wrist in its long, wiry fingers. Jason, who had never seen such an animal, again raised his sword.

"Don't!" she warned. "It's one of her servants, come to fetch us."

The baboon led them uphill at a run, through spiderwebs and briars, over rock outcroppings, fallen logs and cold pools unseen until stumbled through. He left them at the mouth of a cave. Smoke torches lit the way inside. Pausing to pluck burrs from her tunic, Medea looked around, worried. She'd never come this way before and was not sure if this was even part of Circe's palace.

"Enter!"

The imperious whisper seemed so close that both jumped, but they could see no one.

"Enter!" the voice again commanded. When they failed to move, an unseen force pushed them into the passage and propelled them along so fast that they nearly fell with each step. Unseen hands began to pluck at them, tearing away their garments, taking their possessions, until they ran naked and afraid. Medea felt a deathly cold hand pressing into the small of her back. No matter how fast she ran, the painful pressure did not ease, until she stumbled down a step and fell, her arm striking Jason as he fell beside her.

Ghostly light revealed a cryptlike chamber, smooth-walled, narrow and sour-smelling. Beneath them was a grate set into the floor, as if for a drain or the lid of a deadly prison. Directly overhead was total blackness. Torchlight from the passage began to flicker over the walls. When Medea attempted to sit up and see who was coming, a hand pressed her head down into the dust.

"Are we in a cistern?" Jason tried to get to his knees and was also pushed flat and held.

"Lie still," she whispered, as frightened as he but knowing resistance was useless. They had sought Circe and were now in her power.

From the darkness overhead a pig squealed, a shrill,

echoing death scream that ended in a liquid gurgle. Blood, hot and sweet, began to pour down over them, into their faces and hair, becoming denser until they were drenched in gushes of the stuff. And all Medea could think of then was that there was so little difference between the smell of this blood and that of Apsyrtus.

After what seemed forever, the flow ceased. They were yanked to their feet, stunned and dripping, trying to wipe their eyes and nostrils clear. The blood quickly congealed. Both cowered at the sound of Circe's voice from the darkness overhead—he because he guessed who spoke, she because she knew.

"You came here to be purified of betrayal and murder. I have done that. For *you*, Medea, I have sacrificed my sacred white sow. Not because you are deserving of her death, but because of a promise I made to your mother long ago. Now leave my palace, both of you."

"But can't I see you?" Medea begged without thinking.

"No." The answer was cold, inflexible. "You don't want to see me. What you want is my acceptance of this path you've chosen. That I cannot give." She paused, then added more softly, "If, out of my hatred for my brother Aeetes, I had created a malicious enchantment for his favorite daughter, I could not have devised one half so cruel as that you've created for yourself."

The chill that went through Medea then had nothing to do with being wet, naked, and cold. "But I hoped you might be pleased. Aeetes has always been more enemy than brother to you."

"And you were much more to me than his daughter!" The disappointment and anger in the words echoed painfully in the enclosure. "Is this what you will do with your knowledge, Medea?"

Before Medea could reply, the unseen hands grabbed them and pulled them back the way they had come, through the tunnel and back into the night. Their garments were draped over their wet shoulders and their possessions dropped at their feet—as if Circe wanted nothing that was theirs left on her island. A mute servant appeared to lead them to the shore, where a ferryman waited. The ferryman was cloaked in black, his face hidden by a hood, and he, too, did not speak, but simply rowed. On the opposite shore, he gestured for them to get out.

Where he left them in the shallows, they bathed, shuddering with cold and fear. A sand dune was their bed and blanket. Damp as it was, they fell instantly asleep, exhausted.

She was wakened before dawn by crabs clambering over her head, sorting through her hair, nibbling on the pig's blood left by her hurried washing. Jason, too, was being chewed on; she could see the crabs as fist-sized dark spots moving over his blond hair and the sand. She picked them off, throwing them toward the surf, then touched him, as if to smooth his brow. He turned and smiled in his sleep. Any doubt she might have had dissolved in a sudden rush of tenderness and longing. From her bag she took a cloth and tucked it carefully over his hair to protect him, then lay close beside him in the sand and put her arms around him to keep him warm and safe.

He woke her after sunrise with the news that two white horses were tied to a plum tree at the edge of the beach. There were food bags slung over the blankets on their backs. Rolled into one bag was a message. Medea read Circe's bold brushstrokes: "When you reach your destination, my horses will come back to me."

"How will they know the way?" said Jason.

She shrugged, preoccupied by the realization that, for the first time since they'd met, she and Jason would be alone together, and for six days and nights. She smiled up at him, her face aglow. "Six days," she said, "think of it."

"Yes," he said. "We'll need every bit of it if we're going to reach the *Argo* on time."

The coast was wild and rugged. To avoid any possible trouble, they gave wide circle to the few villages they passed. They rode from dawn to dusk through the long spring days, stopping only when the horses needed rest or water. At night they slept on opposite sides of the fire. His sole desire seemed to lie in rejoining his companions and his ship.

It was possible, she told herself, that he was shy of women, or that he believed the purification rite required seven days of chastity, but she was too proud to ask or to will him to want her. Several times she caught him staring at her with the same expression on his face that her father got when Toas read him the tax returns, secretive but well satisfied. She tried to take comfort from that and reminded herself that she also stared at him when he wasn't looking, taking pleasure in the way sunlight made his hair shine, the way his eyes crinkled when he laughed, and in the beauty of his body.

As they rode, he told her stories of the Argonauts' adventures on the voyage to Colchis. Once, he said, they had been attacked with rocks and clubs by six-handed giants, but had beaten them off. At the strait into the Black Sea the *Argo* had nearly been crushed between clashing rocks that rolled and smashed together when a ship tried to pass. Of his companions he said that Orpheus could soothe ferocious animals with the beauty of his music, and even Hercules calmed down when he heard him play. Hercules, he assured her, could kill a man with one blow of his club or fist and had done so many times, although he often regretted the killing when his rage passed.

As she listened to his stories, she got the firm impression that Hercules was not sane and could not be trusted. How was it, then, she wondered, that the other Argonauts spoke so fondly of him? She remembered Atalanta saying that Hercules should have been the *Argo*'s captain. If he was as unstable as Jason implied, why would the others want him as their leader?

For her part, she told him stories from her childhood, especially those her father had told her of Corinth, since Jason seemed particularly fond of hearing those. But when he asked her how much sorcery she knew, she merely smiled and said that most of what people called magic was superior knowledge and discipline and could be learned by study. He didn't believe her and asked how much discipline she had used to put the dragon to sleep. Her reply, "Not nearly all I possess," silenced him for miles.

By the time they reached the small bay where the *Argo* and her crew were waiting, each knew the other somewhat better, or knew what each wished the other to know, but they were still neither friends nor lovers.

Just as they dismounted, violent tremors shook the earth. There was a great rushing sound as from a windstorm, but there was no wind. The horses reared and broke away, throwing off their blankets. They headed east toward home, running wild, with tails and manes flying. Jason fell onto his knees and pleaded with his gods for mercy, but Medea sat down and searched the sky, looking for a hawk, high up—Circe watching over her horses.

Those Argonauts who had not come running to greet them ran now—to escape the high waves that began to pour onto the beach. The *Argo,* which had been pulled well up onto the sand, was lifted by a wave, carried forward, and set down almost at Jason's feet— as if the Earth Mother couldn't wait for him to leave this shore, Medea thought; the companions read it as an omen of divine Hera's forgiveness of Jason.

TEN

THE PARTY HAD GONE ON TOO LONG. Medea slipped away to walk along the cliff top overlooking the sea. Just off the beach below, some of the islanders were night fishing, the torches on their boats golden lights on the black water. She sat on a rock ledge to watch, glad for the quiet and solitude.

The Argonauts were celebrating their return to Greek waters. Most were drunk and had been so since noon, when they had reached the island. The few who were still sober, like Orpheus and Atalanta, had long since gone to bed. Meleager too had disappeared, limping from the hall. Their host, King Alcinous, did not seem entirely pleased by the honor of providing food and lodging for so many rowdy royal guests. Early in the evening he and his queen, Arete, had retired, claiming that merely to hear of the heroes' exploits had exhausted them. "And as for taking Aeetes' daughter as well as the Sacred Fleece . . ." Alcinous had not elaborated on this, but both he and the queen had viewed her with obvious concern.

Medea could understand their exhaustion; she too was tired of listening. If she never heard another song or story of their exploits, she would thank the Goddess for her infinite mercy. It seemed to her she had been listening to the Argonauts do nothing but talk for weeks. The *Argo*'s trip along the Thracian coast and through the Hellespont had been uneventful, thus giving them plenty of free time to tell stories.

In spite of their tales, she had seen no clashing rocks, but only common ice floes, the bobbing remains of the massive icebergs that came down the rivers from Hyperborea each spring. Pushed by rapid currents through the straits, the ice sometimes drifted as far as Troy.

No ships had come out from Troy to challenge the *Argo*'s passage, and she saw none on patrol—which she found as odd as Aeetes had found it. Odder still was the ominous black cloud that had stretched along the horizon where she knew the city to be. Troy had been burning when the *Argo* passed, she was almost sure of that, but she couldn't imagine who would burn so rich a city.

A drunken clamor from the hall interrupted her musing. Overhead an owl gave a peevish hoot, as if irritated by the raucous shouts of greeting. A deep voice bellowed "Silence!" The shouting continued. There was a loud crash of pottery and metal drinking cups, followed by a silence so complete that she could hear the soft voices of the slaves working in the kitchen behind the palace. A wave rushed in onto the rocks below, and then another, as if the ocean too had been muted until now.

She smiled to herself, thinking that lack of sleep had worn thin the king's patience, and she wondered how large the servant was who had been sent to quiet the guests. In any event, she was grateful; if the quiet continued, she would go to bed, sure now of being able to sleep.

Queen Arete had given her their finest guest room, a space some eight feet square, with a couch, water jar, and a slit for a window. But then the palace itself was so small that a lesser noble of Colchis would have used it as a stable. Even so, she had been assigned twelve young slave girls to provide for her comfort. The girls had bathed, oiled and dressed her in a linen gown, stiff and scratchy. They had oiled and combed her hair into the local style—all forehead curls with the back plastered down and wrapped by a linen band. Medea had submitted to this indignity with the hope that Jason might be pleased to see her dressed as a Greek woman. And, indeed, when she had entered the banquet hall that evening, all eyes had turned to her and there had been startled exclamations—but from the comments she overheard, it was her gold jewelry that excited them, not her beauty. And Jason had already been too drunk to do more than smile in her direction as she was seated beside the queen.

A star fell, tracing an arc of light across the northeastern sky. As it disappeared beyond the edge of the sea, she became aware of being watched. Someone or something dangerous was standing in the darkness behind her. The tactile hair rose on her arms and neck, and she shivered.

Getting up casually, as if to see the fishing boats more clearly, she turned. Against the faint light from the palace stood what appeared to be an enormous bear with a grotesque head and ears. A performing animal kept by the palace? She sniffed. The smell was more catlike—a meat eater. But cats never stood erect.

"You are like me." The voice was deep and rumbling, the tone one of puzzled wonder. "You are like me," he repeated. "I can feel it, see it in the air around you. You are a child of the gods."

"And who are you?" she asked softly. A sacred madman, obviously, dressed in some creature's skin, but a madman too large and too close to try to escape from. She touched the stone hanging at her throat and wondered if the man could be willed into submission.

"You don't know me?" He seemed greatly surprised and hurt by her ignorance.

"I can't see you" was her diplomatic reply.

"Ah."

The dark form moved. Living wood creaked and broke. Rocks chinked and sparks flew. Flames licked up and grew bright, and the smell of burning cedar pitch mingled with the salt air. When he raised the flaming fatwood brand, she saw him clearly.

The arm that held the impromptu torch was thicker than her waist. He was nearly seven feet tall and heavily muscled. As a cape, he wore the dried-out, shabby pelt of a huge lion. Its head served as his helmet. His face was framed by the teeth left in the lion's grotesquely dislocated jaws. His nose had been repeatedly broken; his dark eyes were fever-bright. His own dark hair, the dead beast's mane, and his red beard seemed all tangled into one bushy mass. The pelt's forepaws were fastened to his leather breastplate. The hind legs and tail flapped at the back of his bare knees. A belt secured a leather apron at his waist and also held the widest sword she'd ever seen.

"Hercules?" she guessed, remembering the Argonauts' tales.

He smiled and nodded, pleased as a child to be recognized. Then, deciding he had no further need of the light, flung the torch like a javelin toward the sea. Its fiery arc became a second falling star that landed near the fishing boats, provoking frightened shouts.

"I am Medea."

"King Aeetes' daughter?"

"Soon to be Jason's bride."

He stood silent for so long that she became uneasy, then angry because he began to laugh, a wild, rumbling amusement that swelled until she thought he'd wake the island.

"Are you laughing at me?" she asked indignantly when she could make herself heard again.

"No." He sighed, abruptly depressed, as he seated himself on the rock ledge near her and laid his sword beside him. His smell, a mixture of dried blood, woodsmoke, rotting hide, and sweat, was overwhelming, but she thought it best not to show her distaste. "No," he repeated slowly. "I was laughing at Jason. When I saw you, it suddenly became clear to me how he got the Sacred Fleece."

"He won it!"

"They told me you'd been kidnapped," he said.

She frowned. "Who?"

"Aeetes' men. They came to Troy. I let them go. I

had no quarrel with them." The great head swung toward her. "You weren't kidnapped, were you?"

"No."

"And so they will surely follow Jason until—"

"But why? They can't attack the *Argo* here, in Greek waters."

"They won't have to. They will come here and appeal to King Alcinous." He seemed quite lucid now. "Alcinous will be sympathetic. No man, especially a king, likes to lose a daughter to an adventurer. No king as poor as Alcinous would willingly insult a king as rich as Aeetes."

Her hands and feet went cold. "He might give me back to Father's men?"

"Yes."

She'd never thought that Aeetes' power extended so far. "And so you came to warn us, to help us escape? To protect the Sacred Fleece?"

"No. I came to learn how Jason succeeded where I was sure he would fail," he said in his deliberate way. "Now I know; his looks won him the Fleece. And you. Most women love him on sight—as he loves them." He sighed again. "I am thinking someday you will see him clearly. Someday you will need a friend. I will be that friend. You have only to come to me, or send for me. I will help you. You and your children."

This future he foresaw, this anticipated trouble, caused him to stare into the darkness and mumble to himself as if he were alone. She did not dare to interrupt but sat listening. "I know Jason," he said. "I know him very well. Oh, yes! He once swore to be my friend, my companion. Yet when my squire, my beautiful

Hylas, became lost in the woods and Polyphemus and I went searching for him, it was my sworn friend Jason who gave the order to sail without us. My friend Jason left me stranded in Mysia. My friend Jason deserted me. Because the winds were right, he said. As if the winds wouldn't change again."

"I assumed you had left the *Argo* by choice. . . ." She hesitated, guessing that, again, what Jason had said was true, but it was only the part of the truth that was convenient for him. "Perhaps there were other reasons for sailing then?"

"Yes." The claws on the brittle pelt scratched against the rock ledge as Hercules shifted. "Jealousy. It's hard to be captain when your entire crew looks to another man for authority. And then I beat him in the rowing contest. Jason rowed until he fainted from exhaustion. I was still going strong when my oar broke. After the *Argo* was beached, we were looking for a tree, Hylas and I, so I could make a new oar, when Hylas disappeared. I thought the boy had returned to the ship, but he was gone. Gone. Polyphemus found his clothing and water jar beside a spring. But no boy. We called and called. We hunted through the night. And when we got back to the shore—the *Argo* was gone, too."

At that Hercules began to laugh with inordinate loudness, and in his laughter she heard a deeper hint of madness or perhaps total despair. "I promise to be your friend, Medea. We are alike. And because we are—he will betray you as he betrayed me. Remember that, Medea. Remember that none of them will ever forgive us for being what we are. For all their promises, or professed love, or need of us, they will never overcome their resentment and their fear. Because I am too strong, and your knowledge makes you too powerful."

"I'm sorry you feel he betrayed you," she said softly.

He gave no sign that he heard but simply sat facing her for some minutes. She had the uncomfortable feeling that he could see her in the darkness. Then, with no warning, he pushed himself to his feet and took up his sword.

"You came here from Troy?" she said hurriedly, since he seemed about to leave.

"What's left of it."

She had been right; the city *was* burning. "And King Laomedon and his family?"

"Dead." He said the word with satisfaction. "I allowed his infant son to live. His name is Priam now. And his sister. I gave her to Telamon."

"*You* burned Troy?"

"The gods burned Troy," came his self-righteous answer. "Laomedon must have cheated them, too, and in their rage, they shook his walls down so that Telamon and I could march in with our armies. The fires were burning as we marched toward the city." The memory seemed to please him, for he laughed again. "Laomedon cheated me of my horses. But he won't cheat anyone else. Never again." And with that, he walked away in the darkness, still laughing.

"Are you coming with us to Iolcus?" she called after him.

"No. I leave that grief to Jason."

When he had gone, she moved away from the spot where he had been sitting. The smell of him still lingered. In spite of herself, she was shocked by what he'd said. It was not the gods but the Mother Earth's shaking that had broken the walls of Troy and caused the fires, the same earth shaking that had sent Circe's horses on their homeward route. But to think of rich Troy overrun by a barbarian army, the royal family dead except for the infant boy and his sister. She had seen both of them the summer before when she and Chalciope had joined other royal visitors to the summer fair at Troy. Now all that was gone, too.

Hercules offered her loyalty and friendship, which admittedly was far preferable to his enmity, but only time would prove how sincere his offer was. He seemed half mad to her, and for all she knew, his offer may have been simply a way to antagonize his rival, Jason, and undermine his happiness. But Hercules had already done her a kindness in showing her just how vulnerable she was here.

If the Colchians came as he predicted, she would need an ally in this palace. Not the king—he would fear her father's anger. Queen Arete seemed eager to be kind; if she went to her—no, it would be far better if Arete believed the idea was her own.

It took little effort to will the queen to her. When she heard her calling "Princess Medea? Are you out here?" she waited for a second call before answering.

"Wait here," Arete ordered a servant. Footsteps hurried along the path to where Medea waited. "What are you doing out here alone in the night? Did someone insult you? Are you homesick? You must be cold in this dampness." The warmth of the queen's own shawl settled over Medea's shoulders. "I had a vision just now—a dream—that you were out here crying. Isn't that odd? And here you are. Now what is it? Trust me. Speak to me as if I were your mother."

"I'm afraid," Medea whispered. "Alone and afraid."

"You're not alone. I'm here. What has frightened you?"

"My father."

It was difficult to keep the queen from well-intentioned interruptions as Medea explained her very real worries. "If I am taken back to him, Aeetes will kill me. He's fond of killing, slowly, piece by piece." She described some of the more brutish deaths, including torture, burning, and dismemberment, and the one that horrified her most: being put naked into a pit full of hungry rats and sheep ticks.

Queen Arete was a round-faced woman with protuberant eyes, made wider now with horror. "He might do that? To his own child? Well, of course, I do know of one king who put out his daughter's eyes and sentenced her to grind barley to flour. I thought it quite unfair. . . . Are you and Jason married? In the true, physical sense?"

"There's been no time. No privacy. The *Argo*—"

"Jason's probably scared to death of you," the queen said bluntly. "You've a formidable reputation; even *I'd* heard of you. They say you know every drug that grows, every song and spell. I must admit we are fond of gossip here—it passes the time around the fire in winter. But with you being half barbarian and from the edge of the world . . ." She paused and decided to take a more tactful course. "What I mean is, for all your beauty, once Jason had you with him, uh . . . he may have had qualms about actual marriage to a . . . ah. You see"—she altered course again—"my husband might

[*135*]

return a kidnapped virgin to her father, but he could hardly separate husband and wife, especially if the wife had chosen the husband. Now could he?"

"I don't know," said Medea, wondering if Arete had been going to say "marriage to a witch."

"Of course not," Arete said firmly. "I'll summon Jason and make the situation quite clear to him—and then I'll talk to the king. Don't worry; we'll put an end to your fear and loneliness."

At dawn, as Hercules had predicted, the Colchian ships appeared: six blue sails, each emblazoned with a white disk atop three white rays. Seeing the *Argo* on the beach, they landed. According to Medea's servant girls, who proved to be quite informative, the Colchian admiral, Aras, went directly to the king and—after telling him of the Sacred Fleece, the kidnapping of Medea, and the murder of Prince Apsyrtus—demanded Jason's punishment and the return of what had been taken. King Alcinous said he would consider the matter overnight. Prince Jason had been wakened by the queen and told of his enemy's arrival, the girls said; and in spite of a severe pain in his head, he had sent his servant to request a meeting with Medea as soon as possible.

To give him time to consider how he might fare without her help, Medea took a small pouch full of gold and left the palace. Dressed as a local woman, she spent the morning in the city's marketplace. Among her purchases was the mummy case of an Egyptian girl, dusty but exquisite, inlaid with lapis lazuli, precious glass, and shell. The face of the dead girl pictured on the case touched her, and she wondered where and how she had come to this backwater. When her shopping was done, she took the time to accompany her purchases to the *Argo* and see them loaded aboard. Two Colchians watching the ship saw her but did not recognize her.

It was long past noon when she walked back up the hill to the palace. To her great pleasure, and relief, Jason came out to meet her. Taking both of her hands in his, he smiled into her eyes.

"I've been waiting for you." He spoke softly so that the three slave girls with her could not hear. "I have good news! During the night the goddess Hera came to me in a dream. To my great joy, she told me that I am free at last to keep the rest of my promise to you. We will be married tonight."

"Your goddess—or Queen Arete seen through a drunken blur by lamplight?" she said, smiling, but not in the mood for a fanciful story.

"The goddess can assume any form she wishes." He answered without smiling. "I never doubt her aid or her instructions—and you shouldn't doubt my love for you."

They were married that evening, after dark. The affair was kept secret. The wedding hall was a dusty cave on a tiny island just offshore. The only guests were the companions.

To gain privacy and quiet, Medea had drugged the wine and warned Jason not to drink. One by one, the companions pushed their plates and cups aside, pillowed their heads on their arms, and fell asleep at the table. When only a few servants too timid to taste the wine remained awake, Jason took her hand and led her to the marriage bed at the rear of the cave. They were separated from the others by only a leather drape.

[*137*]

Someone had placed the Sacred Fleece over the wedding couch. On seeing it, Medea gave a cry of disgust and threw the ill-omened thing on the floor.

Long after Jason fell asleep, she lay in his arms, listening to his breathing—and from the other side of the drape, his companions' drunken snores. She couldn't help thinking that, had she been married in Colchis, the wedding would have lasted nine full days. Tents would have covered the meadows like flowers. Trumpet fanfares would have announced whole caravans of royal guests from every kingdom and city between Aea and Egypt. All those attending would have brought precious gifts. There would have been elephants and camels, cheetahs on golden chains, slaves and incense and flowers. Nine high priestesses would have conducted an elaborate wedding ritual mystery in the Temple of the Goddess. A public ceremony would have honored her and her husband. There would have been burnt offerings and blood poured onto the earth. Choirs would have sung songs composed for the occasion.

But she had chosen exile and Jason. The Great Goddess ruled, and nothing on earth happened without her knowledge and planning. Therefore, there must be a reason for this dreadful wedding.

In the morning they were summoned before King Alcinous. Queen Arete was there and, waiting in the petitioners' corner, the Colchian admiral, Aras, and two of his captains. The Colchians made signs to ward off evil when they saw Medea enter.

"If the Princess Medea is a virgin, she must be returned to her father." King Alcinous, nervous of confronting either the Argonauts or the Colchians, sternly addressed a limestone column to his right. "If not, she is free to go with her husband."

"She is my wife," said Jason.

"Was the marriage of your own free will?" the king asked Medea.

"It was," she said.

"Then the father has no further claim on the daughter," decreed King Alcinous. "The *Argo* is in Greek waters, subject to Greek law, and thus free to go where it will."

The Colchians groaned in anger and despair. "You have sentenced us to exile!" Aras shouted at Medea. "We can't go home. We were ordered to return with you and the Sacred Fleece or not return at all. And this was *before* you killed your brother, Aeetes' heir. Because of you, a hundred men must lose their homes and families. Because of you, a hundred women will suffer widowhood while their men still live. Because of you, children will lose their fathers and risk being sold into slavery to survive."

"No!" she protested, "not because of me! Because Aeetes failed to keep his promise to Jason!"

But no one listened.

When the *Argo* sailed on the morning tide, she rode lower in the water. Queen Arete had given Medea the twelve slave girls as a wedding gift, saying: "You are the daughter of a great house. You will be queen of Corinth and Iolcus. You can't afford the luxury of travel without servants."

Medea thought *luxury* an odd choice of words but quickly learned what Queen Arete meant. The girls and their belongings jammed the already crowded deck; three of them were afraid of the water and cried; all were seasick within minutes. For most of each day, it was she who took care of them instead of the other way around, and at night she had to protect them from the lecherous attentions of some of the Argonauts.

During the voyage, spring became summer. At each friendly island the Argonauts stopped to trade and tell of their adventures. They were all acclaimed as heroes and entertained, sometimes for days, as the sons of royal houses. Medea herself was the object of endless curiosity. Everyone was eager to see this "witch daughter" of the fabulous King Aeetes the Mighty, this barbarian princess of such unnatural learning and beauty.

Days became weeks and then months, until Medea nearly despaired of the trip ever ending.

ELEVEN

ON AN EVENING IN EARLY AUTUMN, the *Argo* coasted past the shores of Iolcus. The oars were raised, the sail filled by a gentle breeze. In the quiet, the water rippling off the bow made a playful sound. Cooking smoke rose from the villages along the shore. The scent of burning charcoal drifted out across the water. Scattered over the treeless hills were grazing cattle and oxen, hobbled for the night. Flocks of pigeons circled overhead, their wings and underbellies flashing pink in the sun's last rays. On every beach were fishing boats and nets hung up to dry. But there were no people in view.

"Why hasn't anyone come out to hail us?" Jason wondered aloud.

"Perhaps no one has seen us yet," Meleager said. "Or they fear us, not recognizing the *Argo*. We've been away a long time, and we've changed the color of our sail," he reminded the others.

Medea remained silent, taking in the view, the grassy

hills, the tiny fields, the twisted olive trees. A land of dry, poor soil, unlike the rich, deep loam of Colchis. The houses were stone huts, with a goat pen next to each. Was this poor place the kingdom for which Jason and his Argonauts had risked their lives?

As they drew closer to shore, they came upon an old man fishing from a tiny boat. With one hand still grasping his net, he waved a laconic greeting. He had the air of someone who knows life can't do much more to him, good or bad.

"What do you want?" he called when they came within hailing range. "Who are you? You're scaring my fish away!"

"Don't you recognize the *Argo,* old man?" Jason pointed at the Golden Fleece hanging on the mast. "We've freed Iolcus from its curse!"

The old fellow didn't even bother to glance at the Fleece. He gave a derisive snort and turned his attention to his net, where a big mullet was now thrashing. "The *Argo* sank with all aboard," he called as the ship eased nearer. "Went down off Troy or some such foreign place."

"Who told you that?"

"The king, Pelias." He tipped the fish into the bottom of his boat, where it flapped frantically until he clubbed it. With his dinner assured, he could afford to give Jason more attention. "King Pelias said the *Argo*'s loss was an omen that meant he was to go on ruling. He sent his men to the old palace to kill the prisoners, but King Aeson swallowed some poison before they could get him. The queen stabbed herself."

Ignoring the cries of dismay from a few of the Argonauts, as well as Jason's white face, the old man con-

tinued his story. "They had an infant son, you know—
King Aeson and his queen. Born after the *Argo* sailed.
Brother to that boy Diomedes . . . Jason . . . whatever
he called himself. But with him drowned, that baby
would have inherited. Pelias himself killed the baby.
Dashed its brains out on the stone floor. That's when
the queen killed herself. They say she died cursing
Pelias with her last breath—for all the good that did
her."

The old man cast his net again with deliberate care.
"If you have any plans of taking the city, boys, I'd take
a few more men. King Pelias has over three hundred
men in his garrison now. Strong men, fed well and kept
loyal by the favors he shows them." He looked up from
the water. "Even if you were who you claim to be,
they'd take that old fleece from you and feed your livers
to the buzzards."

Jason, who had listened silently to this terrible news,
now grabbed a spar, and with it, reached out and
hooked the old man's boat, jerking it against the side of
the *Argo* with such angry force that the old man nearly
tumbled sideways into the water. "You forget you saw
us or our ship!" Jason ordered. His look and tone was
so fierce that the old man instantly nodded, finally re-
spectful. "If anybody asks, you say we were a barbarian
trader asking for directions." The old man nodded
again. "If you plan to get any older or wiser," Jason
advised, "stay away from the palace for the next few
days."

"Only fools go near the palace now—unless they're
forced to—and then they don't return." The old man
had to show he wasn't completely cowed. "You take my
advice. Go home!"

"I am home," said Jason, and his companions cheered.

They landed in near-darkness on a secluded beach several miles from the palace. After pulling the *Argo* up on the shingle, they assembled for a war council.

"Let's attack the palace now," said Jason, "and kill this lying, murdering Pelias while we can count on an element of surprise." There was general agreement until Meleager spoke.

"We're outnumbered five to one. And it's night, in a strange city. To come so far, to endure so much and return successful, only to risk death now makes no sense. I say we each go home to our own land, each raise an army, and at an agreed-upon time, we all return with our combined forces. Pelias then could choose between surrender or death. He's no fool—he'd surrender."

To this there was enthusiastic approval. All were tired now and dispirited by the lack of any welcome. Most had no quarrel with Pelias; they just wanted to go home.

"Would *you* surrender, knowing that as soon as you did, your enemy would kill you?" asked Jason. "Pelias must die for his crimes against my family."

"It's unfair of you to expect me to be a part of this," said Acastus. "No matter what Pelias has done, he's my father. I won't fight him."

"Does that mean you'll betray us?" Jason's hand went to his sword. Atalanta and Orpheus moved to stop him before he struck Acastus.

"I'll not fight either," said Mopsus. "Not now. Not this way."

"Do the birds teach cowardice?" Jason taunted.

"There's no need for friends to fight." Medea stepped forward into the firelight. She was speaking directly to Jason, but her words were meant for them all. "If you'll let me, I will solve the problem of Pelias—tonight, and without harming anyone else in the palace or city. Rest now and eat as you always do when the *Argo* has been beached. After I've gone, walk down the beach until you can see the palace. Wait there and watch for a torch being waved from the rooftop. At that signal, you'll be free to claim the palace and the kingdom."

Moments before, the Argonauts had been in general agreement that the best thing to do was nothing; now her proposal was greeted with an exchange of resentful glances and hostile questions.

"But how can you do this? By sorcery? By spells? You're not in Colchis; your magic may not work here. If you fail, Pelias will know we're here."

"I won't fail."

Motioning for her twelve slave girls to follow, she set to work. Parcels cached in the *Argo*'s hold were brought out and put beside the fire. She had the girls erect a screen of cloth around the fire and gathered them all inside. Soon a medicinal smell permeated the air.

For more than an hour the companions watched the silhouettes of naked girls moving behind the screen. Gradually the forms changed; hair was loosed from braids and brushed wild; heads were crowned with wreaths; diaphanous cloth draped the slender bodies—except for one, which gradually altered into a bent and twisted crone, dressed in black rags and hobbling on arthritic legs.

When the screen was suddenly dropped, the Argonauts cried out in alarm. The girls had become mad-women, their faces prematurely aged, cheeks and lips bright with Egyptian rouge, eyes glittering with drugs. Six carried green willow whips and unlit torches. The others carried a litter, on which appeared to be a body wrapped in Medea's favorite cloak. Medea was gone, and in her place was a hag with wild white hair and a face collapsed in wrinkles. She cackled with obscene laughter at their shocked expressions, exposing black-ened stumps of teeth. On her chin was a wen with moldlike hairs, and the skin hung on her throat.

Her amusement spent, the hag forced herself to stand erect and slowly surveyed the dumbstruck Ar-gonauts until at last her glance fastened on Jason. He could not meet her eyes. No one said a word. With a sigh, she turned and limped away, leading the dithering slave girls into the darkness.

Not wanting to admit she didn't know where the city was, Medea headed northwest, the direction Jason al-ways faced when he spoke of the palace. She soon came to a rutted road and followed it. The moon rose, red and nearly full. Cicadas sang in the bushes. There were more huts now, scattered along the road like uneven teeth. Then on a hilltop she saw a large building against the horizon and below it a cluster of smaller structures. Iolcus.

She took a deep breath; the air smelled of pine and dust. Whispering a prayer to the Goddess, begging her forgiveness for what she was about to do, she began. From a vial she took a coal and lit the torches. Carrying the blazing lights, the girls went running through the streets, pounding on doors, singing, crying out in weird voices and causing as much noise and commotion as they could.

Dogs began to bark; roosters saw the torches and crowed; cattle lowed nervously. Some goats vaulted the confines of their pens and trotted off into the night. A few kids, curious, joined the wild procession, their neat hooves clattering on the stones, baaing and prancing as if they knew life was all a game. Medea caught a small kid, muzzled it, and hid it inside the mummy case being carried on the litter.

"Wake up! Wake up!" she shouted in a piercing voice made powerful by years of choral practice. "The bad times are ended! Wake up! Welcome good fortune! The Goddess has sent her own image from the far lands to bring good fortune back to Iolcus! Welcome her! Welcome her with wine and wild abandon!"

They were near the palace now. Around her the slave girls yelled and chanted, sometimes drowning her out in their enthusiasm for their roles. As they passed a house, someone emptied a slop jar from the second-floor window, the contents splashing the dust, narrowly missing the crone.

"Beware!" she shrilly warned the black window in the wall above. "Don't profane the Goddess! She will put a curse on you that will make past troubles seem like nothing!"

Men straggled out into the street, some plainly frightened and hiding in the shadows to watch; others—angry at being wakened—had armed themselves with hoes or clubs. Thin children appeared at windows, staring.

She dropped back from leading the procession to

walk beside the litter, and flung back the cover. The torchlight fired off the gold. The eyes, inlays of rich brown agate set into blue white glass, seemed to glow with life. The red lips curved in the benign and remote smile of an Egyptian girl long dead.

"It *is* a goddess!" a man cried. His excited claim was repeated and echoed from house to house and street to street.

"Celebrate!" the madwomen urged. "Welcome her return!" And they passionately embraced the men and kissed them.

"Your king! Your king! The Goddess comes to meet your king!" the hag cried. At her signal, the girls began to sing, a high, wailing chant from the tribes beyond the high Caucasus. She knew these Greeks wouldn't understand the words; it was the effect she wanted, the melancholy mystery, the powerful loneliness that pervaded the music. "Louder!" Her whisper was harsh. "I want them to feel the power of the Goddess! Louder! With authority!"

At the palace gate, she walked past the intimidated guards by crying "Waken the king! The Goddess comes to greet him!" in a voice that echoed back from the walls of the inner courtyard. "No mortal man can stop her!" The girls screamed a berserk accompaniment and struck wildly at the guards with their whips until the confused men dived for cover.

Once inside, Medea paused for only a moment to orient herself. She was in a torchlit, high-ceilinged entry. Through a doorway to the right were steps. At the top of the stairs she could see an ornately gilded red leather curtain hung across a doorway. A curtain fit for a king. She ran up the steps with an ease extraordinary for one who looked so old. She thrust aside the drape and nearly bumped into a man clad only in a loincloth—and that being hastily tied on. She raised her torch and saw him back away, cowering, his eyes darting from her to the mummy case to the wild women crowding in behind her.

"I am King Pelias. How dare you violate my privacy? Guards!"

This was Pelias? This short graybeard with the belly and flabby arms? Once again appearance belied reputation.

"Who are you? What do you want of me?" he demanded nervously.

"You have no need of guards, my son." She spoke softly, so that he was forced to concentrate on listening. "You have no need to fear. You have been blessed by good fortune. The Goddess herself has come from the far and foggy land of Hyperborea to honor your success." Her voice gained strength now, and her tone became hypnotic. "Come from the land of ice and snow in a chariot drawn by fiery serpents, come flying through the nights and days, speeding over plain and mountains, spring and summer and autumn. Come this vast way to see *you* and bring new life for Iolcus. New life for Pelias. Rebirth. Youth." She signaled to the girls to stand the mummy case erect.

"What—" His voice cracked, and he reached for the water pitcher on the stand beside his sleeping couch. "What do you want?"

"Only to reward you," came the soft reply. "The Goddess knows what sacrifice you have made to free Iolcus from its curse. She comes to reward you for your piety. So that you might richly enjoy the rebirth she will bring to your land, she will make you young again, rejuvenate you so that you may sire sons to replace Acastus—who so tragically died in a shipwreck off the coast of Libya."

"My son is dead? Truly?" His question contained more surprise than sadness at the thought.

"Father? What is it? Do you need our help?" Three young and pretty girls pushed their way into the room and to his side. "What is this? Who are these whores?"

His daughters had more courage than the guards, Medea thought as she studied these unexpected members of Pelias's household; they were braver and probably more intelligent. But then they had much more to lose if she was the enemy.

Pretending to ignore the girls as they questioned their father, she quickly took the torches from the wall and planted them in the cracks of the stone floor and lit them so that the light flickering in Pelias's eyes would make it difficult for him to see what else she did. She next sent two of her girls outside to make sure that no other unexpected visitors came in, giving one of the girls a dagger, with orders to kill, if necessary, quickly and quietly.

"You can't believe all this, Father," one of the daughters was saying. "You have never worshipped the Goddess."

"But I always respected her, Alcestis," said Pelias. "And if she chooses to reward me—"

While his attention was distracted, Medea turned her back and carefully slit and loosened the painted wax masking her face, hands and feet. She pushed back the wig so that it would all slide quickly into the hood of her ragged cloak, then loosened the blackened beeswax on her teeth and swallowed it.

"Old hag!" Pelias called. She shuffled around to face him. "My daughters . . . I don't believe that you—"

He paused, distracted by her hands as she began to make odd waving motions around her face and body. She gave a painful little gasp; her hands flew up to cover her face. Slowly she stood erect and as she did so, her ragged cloak slid off and she stepped out of the garment, naked in her youth and beauty.

Both the king and his daughters cried out in surprise, and the girl he had called Alcestis murmured, "How lovely she is," even as she reached for a robe and threw it at Medea's feet.

"Such is the power of the Goddess," Medea said reverently, gratefully, ignoring the robe. "I am made young again. Supple again!" With great deliberation, she touched her face, her arms, her body, as if to assure herself of the transformation. "If she can make an ancient, crippled hag young again, think what she can do for a man as strong and virile as you appear to be," she said, smiling at Pelias.

"She could do this for me?"

"She will do this for you."

Alcestis leaned closer to Pelias and whispered in his ear. He nodded thoughtfully. "It's not that I mean disrespect," he said then, "but I need some proof—other than your own transformation."

Medea feigned amazement. "You can't believe what you have just witnessed?" When he shook his head, she looked away at a far corner of the room, like a cat watching invisibles. "Very well," she said slowly, "the

Goddess has agreed to another demonstration of her power. As her priestess, I must ask you to have your slaves bring me the oldest goat they can find. I'll need copper basins. . . ."

She told him the equipment she wanted, and Pelias agreed to it all without question. She was amazed at the ease of his cooperation, but then reminded herself that she was promising a new life to a cruel and selfish man; of course he would cooperate if there was any chance that what she promised was real.

A servant soon led in a ram so old it wheezed. Its teeth were worn to stumps, and its ribs stuck out beneath its mangy hide. The musky smell of it filled the room. Medea was shocked to see just how poor the kingdom must be for anyone to keep such an animal alive.

"If your Goddess can rejuvenate that wretched thing, I'll believe she can do the same for me." King Pelias laughed nervously, as if suspecting a hoax but hoping against common sense that she spoke the truth.

In answer, she began to chant and dance before the ram, repeatedly touching its head and neck. The animal suddenly staggered. As it fell she knelt, cradling it gently, positioning it so that Pelias could see that it still breathed. From beneath her robe on the floor she took a knife and slit the ram's throat. The ram went on breathing, unaware that its life was draining into a basin.

Rising, Medea resumed her dance, slowly, seductively, still chanting. Pelias watched her with rapt attention, although now and then he would glance down at the ram. From a packet concealed in her hand the dancer sprinkled sleeping powder over him and his daughters. She had to circle them three times before they began to yawn and lose track of what was happening. As she circled past her slave girls she whispered orders, making her whispers seem part of her ritual chant.

Each time she passed the designated statue of the Goddess she knelt. Now, kneeling behind the mummy case, she opened the lid and picked up the baby goat. With one hand clasped over its muzzle so that it couldn't bleat betrayal, she hugged the frightened little creature close.

Making sure one of her girls was always between her and Pelias, she danced faster, chanted louder, until she could safely signal the girls who were to dispose of the dead ram. When she saw it slide away into the shadows, she set the kid on the floor and ended her performance with a shout.

"Behold! The ram has been reborn!"

The kid staggered on its delicate legs, bewildered by the noise and dopey from lack of air, then bleated loudly and trotted over to nuzzle Pelias' bare knees.

"By the gods!" The half-drugged king picked up the kid and examined it closely. "There's no trickery. It's alive. It's real!" He held this proof out to Alcestis. She took the kid and tried to look at its eyes but it struggled to be put down.

"Do you consent to accept the Goddess's gift? Do you want youth again?"

"Not as young as all that," he said, laughing. "I don't want to be an infant. I need to be as strong as I was at sixteen and as powerful and wise as I am today."

"You will be just as you deserve to be," she assured him. "The Goddess will enlist the aid of your own daughters so that you feel you are in safe hands."

Pelias, dull-witted from the soporific, eager to be young again, lay on his couch as he was told to do. He drank the drugged wine without protest and at Medea's touch, went into a profound sleep in which he would feel nothing.

"The Goddess demands the aid and participation of children of his own blood in his rejuvenation," she told his daughters. "Only you can make the sacred opening that will free his body of his old blood and allow the magic infusion I will give him to be effective. What a man sires in his lifetime determines his immortality."

"I won't do it," Alcestis said quickly. "You are asking me to kill my own father."

"Will you deny him what he so richly deserves?" Medea said. "Do you want to see the grief in his face when he wakes and finds he is still old and weak?"

"I will do it," one of the younger daughters said tearfully.

"I'll help you," said her sister.

Sobbing with fear and grief as they did so, they cut their father's throat, and his life began to drain into a copper basin. So that they would not see him die, Medea escorted them from the room.

"You must go up to the roof now and pray to the Goddess in her old moon phase. Take these torches so that you will have light when I call you, and you can run back down these rough steps and see your father as he will be."

Alcestis refused to go, but her sisters begged her.

Finally, because there was little time, Medea took the youngest girl's arm and led the three of them to the roof. Saying that she had to hurry back to attend the king, she left them, waving their torches, chanting prayers, and weeping in the moonlight.

On the beach the Argonauts saw the torches signaling from the palace roof. With a whoop of excitement, they gathered up their weapons and ran toward the city. Armed though they were, they met no resistance. The few who recognized them stared in horror, then ran away, thinking they were a band of ghosts come back from their watery grave to wreak vengence on Pelias for sending them on a fatal quest.

To Medea, waiting in Pelias's room with the twelve slave girls, expecting that the palace guards might come in at any moment, it seemed hours until she heard Jason's voice in the hall below. Footsteps clattered up the steps, and then he burst into the room. One glance at Pelias and Jason gave a glad shout. He swept her up into his arms, almost crushing her in his joy.

"She's saved a hundred lives tonight!" he yelled to his companions. "She's given me sweet revenge for Pelias's murder of my family! You can't deny it; it's Medea who's made our quest successful!"

The Argonauts all cheered her and in their enthusiasm hugged and kissed the slave girls. The girls, with the effect of the drugs they'd taken earlier now wearing off, smiled blearily, exhausted from their evening.

"My poor father!" A wail of grief and loss cut through the jubilation. Acastus dropped onto his knees at seeing his father's body on the royal couch. As the room went completely quiet in respect for his loss, light, hurrying footsteps could be heard approaching, and his sisters appeared in the doorway, Alcestis in the lead. Her startled glance flicked over the crowd, but she paused only an instant before bravely pushing her way in, saying, "We are Pelias's daughters."

"Look!" cried Acastus, "see what this Colchian witch has done to our beloved father!" He leaned aside so that Alcestis could see the still body and the copper basin brimming with dark blood.

Alcestis looked, and as she did so, the two younger girls saw, too; both began to scream. Alcestis made no sound, but turned and looked at Medea with pure hatred. "You murdered him." Her voice was dull with true grief. "Worse, you tricked my poor sisters into doing your ugly deed for you." And, swift as light, she pulled a knife from the sleeve of her robe and swiped at Medea, who jumped aside and evaded a thrust, while Meleager caught Alcestis and held her.

"You tricked my sisters into doing this?" Acastus pushed back his father's head so that the neck wound gaped open. "You let her convince you to do this?" he demanded of the miserable girls. "You're banished! Now! Before the night ends, you'll leave this palace!" He leaped to his feet.

"That's unfair!" Medea said. "You shouldn't punish them. They believed they were helping him. You have no right—"

"*You* have no rights here!" cried Acastus. "I am my father's heir, and I will banish them for their crime." And he pushed the two unfortunate girls out of the door and shouted for the palace guards.

"As wife of Jason, the rightful king of Iolcus, I am the queen of this land," Medea reminded him. "How did you expect Jason to regain this throne without harm coming to your murdering father?"

"Pelias would have honored his promise," said Acastus.

"Yes. The same way he did when he said the *Argo* had sunk and that was his omen to kill Jason's father, mother, and infant brother." Even as she spoke, she was wondering why she had to say this, why Jason wasn't defending her and himself.

"We might have given Pelias the chance to see if he would step aside," one of the Argonauts said, and another added: "Think of the shock and grief to our friend Acastus, seeing his father like this. And to learn his own sisters held the knife."

Medea saw Acastus glance from face to face, saw his expression subtly alter from angry grief to calculated indignation. His next words came as no surprise to her.

"Do you think the people of Iolcus will accept you as king—a man who gained the throne through the deceitful treachery of a *woman*?" said Acastus. "You may be Aeson's son, Diomedes, but you are a total stranger. You've never lived here. No one knows you. My father's army won't support you. If the people rebel against you, which they surely will when they know, you will either have to take your witch-bride and flee into exile or be killed."

Medea looked up at Jason, thinking that surely he would speak out now, but he seemed bemused and was looking at the floor, listening.

"This evening," she said then, "when I volunteered

to solve the problem of King Pelias and harm no one else while doing so, you all agreed. Not one of you said no; no one tried to stop me."

"I didn't agree," said Acastus. "I wouldn't commit patricide."

"But you didn't protest when I came here," Medea reminded him.

No one else said a word.

"I speak for what is best for Iolcus," Acastus said then, "not for myself. After all, we went on this quest to return the Sacred Fleece to its proper shrine—we risked our lives for the welfare of this kingdom. If our return brings war, then what have we accomplished?"

There were cautious murmurs of agreement to this, and Acastus stood up straighter, more confidently. "In the morning, if you are all agreed, we will let the Iolcan Council decide who shall rule." And at the first nod of agreement from the companions, Acastus added, "And now my sister and I must have some privacy so that we might weep for our dead father."

By late afternoon of the next day, Medea herself was weeping.

She sat alone on a large rock at the edge of the sea. She was alone because none of the Argonauts could look her in the eye. The locals fled from her, afraid she would bewitch or kill them, or both. The story of the night before had spread quickly through the town.

From the hill behind the beach came sporadic shouts and cheers, the neigh of horses, and trumpet fanfares. Wisps of oily smoke drifted up from a pyre near the hilltop. The funeral games of Pelias were in progress, and all of Iolcus was there.

Distracted from her misery by an unusually loud cheer, she turned and looked over her shoulder, but even by shading her eyes, she couldn't see what had taken place. Dots of white and brown moved over the grass—slaves and women carrying food and wine up to the feast tables and bringing empty trays and vessels back to the food carts.

She suspected this funeral feast was the first time in a long while that most of these people had had all they wanted to eat. The Argonauts swore the country was poor because the gods cursed it, but from what she observed, the curse of Iolcus was its poor soil and the people's ignorance.

In a land of sparse rainfall, they had cut down all the forests to make charcoal. They dug no reservoirs, had no irrigation channels. They fired the fields each spring rather than plow the stubble under, let animal waste rot in flyblown middens rather than spread it on the fields. Animal waste was impure, they said. Each spring at planting time, most of the men escaped to sea to be pirates and fishermen rather than help with the farming. And they blamed the gods for their poverty? She sniffed with contempt at the thought.

The funeral games and feast today were the first act of the new king of Iolcus—Acastus, son of the usurper Pelias. His second act had been to announce the decision of the Iolcan Council to banish Jason and Medea forever from Iolcus, as soon as the funeral games were ended. And Jason had accepted this without protest.

For some reason, she suddenly remembered Alcestis' eyes as the girl turned from seeing her father's body—the hatred in those eyes. And the cheering had stopped.

Surely Jason knew she had killed Pelias just for him? That she had used the name of the Goddess to play a shameful trick? That she had done this only out of love for him? He didn't seem to care. Or to care about her. More tears threatened. Determined to stop crying, she shook her head and brushed her hair away from her face. He did love her, she told herself; his oath was sincere. But why was he acting this way?

Granted, after seeing this kingdom, she thought it a poor place. But why should he give it up so easily? Lose it both for himself and for their children to come? Corinth would go to their firstborn, but there was no reason why Iolcus couldn't have gone to a second son or daughter when the time came.

She heard a voice above the sound of the waves and wind, and turned; her heart gave a little leap of gladness at the sight of Jason running over the shingle toward her.

"Did you see him?" he called as he waded into the water to join her on the rock. "Meleager won the javelin throw. Thanks to your healing skills, he beat me—and everyone else. Did you see? It was a wonderful throw!"

"No." She moved over just slightly to make room for him as he climbed up to sit beside her. His face was flushed with wine and exercise, and he smelled of crushed sweet grass from the field.

"Oh." He risked a sideways glance at her. "Why are you here alone?" He reached out and took her small hand in his large callused one. "The banishment doesn't begin until we wish to leave. Acastus is just doing what is expected of him. You can't—"

"Why are you acting as if you don't care?" she burst out. "I killed Pelias for you—for his crimes against your family—so that you could have Iolcus! And you give it away! You let him call me "witch." You act as if I mean nothing to you when your comrades turn their backs on me. As if you were ashamed of me. If you love me, how can you do this?"

"Because I do love you," he said softly. Tears brightened his eyes. "I do love you. But we are only two against many. And as you saw last night, the Argonauts are not true friends to me—or to you, either. I could not count on their support if I defied Acastus. I did not want you harmed in the heat of the situation. Iolcus isn't worth more grief to me. It nearly killed me once; it's taken all that was mine—without my ever having lived here. More than ever I saw last night that this is an ill-omened place for me, better left to Acastus. He is a good man—compared to his father.

"I know what you did you did only for me, and I will be forever grateful. But you are the rightful queen of Corinth now and, since I am completely yours, I want more than anything else to be Corinth's king. Your king. Perhaps, because I was surprised by the companions' sympathy for Acastus—I was too silent last night. I beg you to forgive me. Please?"

With that, he took both her hands in his and looked deep into her eyes; his face was naked with love and contrition. And—because the gods wished it—she forgot her anger and disappointment in him and forgave him with a kiss.

"When we sail tomorrow, it will be the last voyage of the Argonauts as a company," he said as they walked back to the hill together. "We will take the Fleece back to its shrine. You will have the honor of putting it back in its proper place—that we've all agreed upon. Then some of the companions will leave us, walking back to their homes. The others will stay with the *Argo* until she reaches their home shore. And you and I will go to Corinth, to our true kingdom."

PART TWO

TWELVE

Half hidden by a shutter, Corinthus watched the motley procession approach and distractedly worried a hangnail on his thumb until pain made him look down and irritably wipe away blood. He was nervous, but not impressed by what he could see of his visitors.

The daughter of Aeetes had begged leave to visit her father's ancestral palace. She had sent gifts ahead, things suited only to a woman or the effeminate men of the East—tiny jars of precious oils and unguents, opium honey, perfume suspended in creamy wax, wines, and a robe of soft blue wool.

Had her visit been official, he told himself, the daughter of a king as mighty as Aeetes was reputed to be would have put on some show of wealth and pomp. But she had not—which suggested that the gossip was true; she had run away or been kidnapped by the son of the old king of Iolcus. It was said the pair of them had taken the Sacred Fleece back to its shrine. And Corinthus had also heard that she was a powerful sorceress.

But if that were true, she could have come here anytime, in the guise of a raven, or an owl, or a hawk, without bothering to send gifts.

As a mark of respect for her father, perhaps he should have sent his chariot to meet her on the beach. But that might have given her the impression of weakness or toadying—in case she felt she had any claim to this land. Even if she did, Aeetes and his might were far away. Besides, Aeetes had been gone so long that he was just a myth to the local people, the king who ruled the edge of the world, the land of the rising sun.

As for the fabled Argonauts, if these men coming up the path were examples, they looked as shabby and sun-bleached as the sails on their ship. They'd be no match for his soldiers. If they provoked a fight. If they behaved themselves, since some were the sons of neighboring kings, it was only common sense to be hospitable. Sometime he might need them as allies.

This girl was expecting to meet Bunus. Indeed, her gifts had been meant for him, as was her note. But he'd sent old Bunus to his tomb almost a year before. It had seemed a waste to him that Bunus should enjoy a regency and a palace while a general as able and ambitious as himself had to do without. No one had opposed him. No one had ever told Aeetes.

Halfway up the hill, Medea stopped to catch her breath and look around. Because she'd seen other Greek palaces, this one didn't shock her. Still, she was disappointed; only the view was as grand as her father's memories of the place. The building looked more like a crude hill fort than a palace. A fence of piled stones enclosed what served as a courtyard. There were stables to one side. Goats roamed at will and used the midden to leap onto the rooftops.

Two men in coarse linen robes came out to meet and escort her into the audience chamber. Medea couldn't tell if they were servants or officers, since they did not introduce themselves. They said only that Bunus was dead; Corinthus ruled in his place.

In the dreary hall that smelled of damp ashes and past meals, Corinthus sat waiting for her behind a pink marble table that had seen better times. He appeared quite old, at least thirty, narrow-faced. His thin blond hair was shot with white. Over his leather tunic he wore the pale blue robe she'd sent. The robe was gathered on the right shoulder by a golden bracelet—a dolphin with blue sapphire eyes. She recognized it as the gift Aeetes had sent Bunus as a reward for his loyalty.

When he saw her, he smiled, almost in spite of himself. The smile deepened the lines of discontent around his mouth and cold gray eyes. He rose and came around the table to greet her, suddenly friendly.

"How sad that old Bunus could not live to see you," he said when the formal greetings were through. "He would have relished the honor of welcoming the beautiful daughter of his old friend and comrade. Bunus's high regard for your father was equaled only by Aeetes' trust in him—or so I'm told." His pause was an apology. "There was, unfortunately, never time for me to get to know Bunus well. His last illness was mercifully short."

"Was he often ill?"

"Several times," Corinthus said vaguely. "Rule by a

sick man invites intrigue. When his death was near, as general of his army, I chose to take his place."

"The people must have been grateful to avoid the uncertainty of waiting for Aeetes to appoint a new regent," she said tactfully, aware of the Argonauts' vulnerability, as well as her own.

Beside her Jason shifted restlessly, ignored up to this point. She took his hand and smiled up at him, the picture of a modest wife relying on the disciplined strength and courtesy of warriors.

"My father has told me so many stories of Corinth," she said, turning back to their host. "Because he's never stopped missing his boyhood home, I would like to know this house and these hills as well as he did, so that I might love them, too. I would be grateful if you could consider me your guestfriend while Prince Jason accompanies the remainder of the Argonauts back to their homes before returning for me."

"And then where will the pair of you go?" Corinthus's tone was carefully casual.

"To his kingdom," Medea said.

Corinthus nodded, satisfied by his assumption. "I would be honored to have Aeetes' daughter as my guest."

For all his initial rudeness, Corinthus proved to be a gracious host. Medea was given the queen's apartment; like Bunus, Corinthus had no wife. He assigned slaves to help her twelve girls and to spy on all thirteen. When he could, he went with her on her daily rides; when otherwise occupied, he sent an armed escort to ride with her.

His spies reported nothing of the witch about her but the same odd and unwomanly habits he himself had observed: She would dismount in a field to pick up a handful of freshly plowed soil and smell it; she wanted to see the olive orchards and the vineyards, and how the grapes and olives were pressed, and where the wine and oil were stored; she asked what grains were grown and why; she watched fishermen hauling in nets and went to see what kind of fish were taken.

She talked to anyone and everyone, slave or freeman, questioning them about their work and their knowledge of the land. A few had heard she was the daughter of King Aeetes. Some of the old people remembered his name and asked if he was coming back—to which she always answered no. But if Aeetes had no interest in returning, why was she so obviously sizing up the potential wealth of the land? Corinthus wondered.

As he studied her, so she studied Corinthus. Although unmarried, he seemed to desire neither boys nor women, his passions being wealth and power. The only noblewomen in the palace were his aged mother, a widowed aunt and the sisters he had given as wives to two of his generals. He was a stern man, not given to generosity, and had a tendency to belittle others. He had traveled little and was impressed only by things Greek, dismissing all else as "effeminate" or "barbarian."

His most precious possession was a Minoan dagger with a hilt of gold and lapis lazuli. Noting that, she gave him a heavy gold collar studded with lapis of the deepest blue. To keep the metal from chafing his throat, the collar was lined with butter-soft leather. Delighted by her gift, he wore it constantly. He invited her to take her meals with him, saying, "My women wouldn't be much company for a young and vital woman like you."

Like Aeetes, he found her a good listener and soon was confiding things to her that he'd never in his life told anyone. Within days he was suggesting, only half in jest, that her choice of a husband had been a mistake. "If you'd only waited," he said, "you could have ruled your father's land with me." At which she smiled but made no comment.

Several weeks after her arrival, Corinthus went hunting. On their return the entire hunting party fell ill. The court doctor could do nothing. Medea was very concerned. The bear they had killed had eaten poisonous berries, she claimed, and by eating its raw liver, they had ingested pure poison. To prove her point, she gave some of the meat to a dog. The dog promptly began to retch and vomit, as the men were doing. Begging Corinthus to allow her to use her medical skill to help, she made up an herbal potion, which she said was a common Colchian remedy.

First the dog and then Corinthus's men tried the potion and soon were well. Corinthus, who had eaten a larger portion of the meat than the others, rallied, but only briefly, and his physician insisted on taking over again. When the doctor's cures and sacrifices to the gods proved ineffective and Corinthus's condition rapidly worsened, Medea begged permission to be his nurse, for which Corinthus was grateful. More than once he whispered that he had at last found the one woman he might have married.

Under his mother's watchful gaze, Medea made him gruels and broths. She fed him, or held his head as he sipped, but he could keep nothing down. His mother tasted everything her son tasted, with no ill effect.

As he weakened, he sent both women from his rooms and called his council to his side. Should he die, he said, and assured them he didn't intend to, he wanted them to make Medea their queen. As Aeetes' child and heir, the people would accept her; there would be no bloody fight for the throne, and with Jason as their king, not only Iolcus but the kingdoms of all the Argonauts would be allies of Corinth. The council, unaware of what had taken place at Iolcus, agreed. Then, to the horror of the watching men, Corinthus began to vomit blood.

When he had recovered enough to speak, he called in Medea and, with the last of his strength, put on her right forefinger the seal ring of red gold that her father had long ago given Bunus. She wept, and the watching council assumed her tears came from true grief. The hand that held her wrist was cold and dry, and as she felt the weak grip loosen, Corinthus sighed, as if with contentment. His eyes went on fondly regarding her even as they glazed.

Corinthus's bronze greaves, his precious dagger, and the collar of gold and lapis were put into a small brass casket, to be placed in his tomb with his ashes. His mother and sisters prepared the body for the pyre. They did not notice that the band of leather lining the gold collar was unduly oily considering the short time the piece had been worn.

On a day gray with autumn rain, Jason returned and beached the *Argo* for the last time. As he was making the sacrifice of a ram and dedicating the ship to his gods, he could see the black smoke of a funeral pyre rising from a hill beyond the palace. A delegation came to meet him and proclaimed him king of Corinth.

The first month after Jason's return was idyllic. Mornings were spent with the council or in the judgment hall, but each afternoon they went riding on the beaches or over the hills. After wine and supper, they spent their nights in love and talk and dreams. For the first time in her life, Medea was aware of being happy; Jason was the friend and lover she had dreamed of long ago. To be with him like this made everything she had ever learned or done worthwhile, because all had led to this time and place and man. She wanted to give him the world but, failing that, to give him a rich and powerful kingdom. She was sure that together they could make Corinth all he deserved. The land could be renewed; the sea was close on either side for fishing and for trade.

With her head on his shoulder, she outlined a dozen different plans—all of which he would have to initiate, since these Greeks, unlike Colchians, would not obey a woman as they would a man.

Jason was content with her planning, so long as she didn't bother him with administrative details. His boyhood with Chiron had taught him how to hunt and ride and fight, how to sing and tell a good story, but not how to govern men or manage a large estate. Nor did he want to learn such boring things.

"You can make Corinth an enchanted kingdom," he told her, "by the sorcery of your smile alone. Together we'll make the land so rich the gods themselves will smile. But buy some clerks; don't expect me to tally accounts."

Had she had time to think about it, that first winter in Corinth would have seemed miserably cold and damp, but she had no time. She had too much work to do.

The men on the palace staff and in the garrison were accustomed to spending their winter days either hunting or by the hearth, drinking, gambling, wrestling, and complaining. They complained about the weather, the food, their boredom, and the laziness of women and slaves. The slaves, bondsmen, and women were used to being cold, hungry, and overworked. Charcoal and wood had to be carried in, ashes carried out, water heated, food prepared, goats milked, cheese made, wool spun, and always butchering done in the snow and rain of the muddy courtyard. After much urging on Medea's part, Jason ordered the men to work.

Improvements began in the courtyard. She had a new barn and stable built at the bottom of the hill and all the livestock moved down there. She had the midden carted off and the manure spread on the palace fields. There was bitter grumbling at this, mutterings that the barbarian daughter of Aeetes was deliberately defiling the purity of Greek land.

Part of the old stable was razed and the rest used as a woodshed. Dry fuel eliminated some of the smoke inside the palace, as did shutters in the windows along with leather curtains and windscreens. Charcoal was burned only where its deadly smoke could vent. This command also caused complaints.

Lacking enough men to build a decent reservoir, she

had Jason order the garrison to drain and clean all the wells and cisterns. Where possible, she redesigned both to filter the water intake through holding tanks of charcoal and clean gravel. Following the design of the Dawn Palace, trenches were dug and vitreous water pipes made and fitted to supply the living quarters, the kitchens, and the new stable with running water and covered drains.

Word got around in Corinth that this was the queen's idea, since she had been seen drawing the network of pipe placement and explaining to the warriors and workmen what had to be done. To their surprise and general disapproval, she supervised all the work—with Jason at her side.

This modernization, already old in her part of the world, caused both wonder and hostility among free Corinthians, but it endeared her to the kitchen and stable slaves, whose lives she much improved.

When spring came again and it was realized that, for the first time in memory, no one in the palace had died of cold or fever during the winter, people credited their new king with their good fortune. Jason publicly agreed. The harvest that year bore out the truth of his claim.

Medea was fourteen that summer when Medeius was born. Both he and Argus, born the following spring, looked like her. Jason jokingly called them "my little barbarians" and, though pleased they were sons, was otherwise indifferent to them. She often wondered if he would have shown more interest had they been blond.

In warm weather, men were set to work on the palace. Much of the roof had to be replaced, the rooms replastered and whitewashed. Two slave artists were set to painting murals on the walls. She taught her slave girls to make beehives of rope and then to teach the craft to children and enlist their aid in finding wild beehives for taming. She had reservoirs and irrigation ditches dug and orchards of olives and fruit trees planted. Little by little, Corinth began to prosper.

Jason grew restless. He was tired of spending his mornings in the judgment hall, his afternoons supervising the endless work. The weather was fine, and he wanted to go to sea again, away from all this tedium. But the other Argonauts had work to do at home and were not interested. He amused himself riding about Corinth on a tall roan stallion that had once belonged to Bunus or visiting nearby kingdoms, leaving his duties for Medea to handle. Often he would return with guests, younger men still adventuring. While Medea made them welcome, she sometimes resented the food, wine, and care they cost, with their endless hunts and contests and drunken evenings—to say nothing of Jason's time lost to her. But she blamed the guests, not Jason, for the length of their visits.

Two years passed happily enough, then four. Life assumed an even tenor. The weather was kind, the rain adequate. With plentiful grass, more lambs and kids were born. The grain and olive harvests were good, as was the production of honey. People had enough to eat and could still pay their taxes and have some left over for trade. In the village a bakery opened, then a glassworks and a kiln. Vitreous tile became a trade item.

With prosperity, Medea had an old section of the palace razed and the stone used to build a grand new hall with a pool large enough to bathe in, complete with fountain, waterfall, and a stream which led outside into the terraced garden below the palace. As a gift for Jason, she had a chariot built that was as fine as her father's. She traded one of her best gold necklaces for a matched team of white Cilician horses. As an added gift, their daughter was born, a beautiful baby as blonde as her father. They named her Eriopus. To Medea's mild surprise, Jason showed no more interest in this child than he had in the others.

By the fifth winter, after another son, Alcimedes, was born, Medea had enough free time to be aware that she was lonely among these Greeks. There was no one with whom she could talk as a friend and equal. Jason spent most of his time now with his men. The women were subservient creatures living a life apart, secluded not by walls but by endless work and ignorance. Besides, they neither liked nor trusted her and called her the barbarian when they thought she couldn't hear. There were her slave girls, of course, the gift of Queen Arete, but one didn't make friends of slaves, even in desperation. One by one, she arranged good marriages for them.

It was to shut out the loneliness that she resumed her studies. She had a large room built, with storage shelves and tables, two hearths, a kiln, and an urnlike vessel that served as a crude vacuum chamber. Gradually the shelves filled with containers of everything from odd mushrooms and lichens to ergot-blackened grain, sands, stones, and the ashes of old bones, which glowed green in the dark. There, too, in a hidden niche, she kept the black chest that had been Circe's gift.

When she was out in the hills collecting supplies,

each cry of a hawk or eagle made her search the sky with hope that Circe was up there, watching. But if any of the birds were more than birds, she saw no sign of that. Circe had not punished her, but she'd not forgiven her either. And her warnings about Jason, like all the similar warnings, had not come true. He had not betrayed her; she still loved him dearly, and their children seemed especially precious to her because they were his.

Sometimes she thought of her father. Did Aeetes always feel as she did now, that he lived in lonely exile? And had they dared to tell him just how his son had died? That he'd lost two children to Jason? She tried never to think of Apsyrtus, but he came to her in dreams, his eyes bewildered and afraid, the waves closing over his face. Sometimes she dreamed of Alcestis as the girl looked at her dead father, and of Pelias and Corinthus—he had become so trusting. She would waken in a sweat and get up and go work in her study.

The summer her daughter was three, Medea went into the hills one afternoon to gather wild peony for medicine. Only her older children were with her; the baby and nurses had been left behind. Binding a sheaf of plants with a vine, she stood watching the children roll down a grassy bank, one after the other. They played with the abandonment of puppies, and she smiled to see their joy. At the base of the slope they jumped to their feet, giggling with dizziness, and staggering, then, one by one, they went still and stared openmouthed at something behind her.

Thinking they saw an animal and not wanting to

startle it into attack, she gripped her digging knife and slowly turned around. What met her eyes was more dangerous than any animal.

Hercules stood there, his hood and lion's cape black with dust and old blood. He clutched his spear like a walking stick, and its worn blade flashed red gold. From the shadow of the lion's skull, his eyes burned with fatigue. The madness she had sensed before was more evident now. His throat moved as if he were carrying on an angry internal dialogue, obsessed by old injustices. She couldn't be sure he recognized her, or even that he saw her.

"Children, we are honored. This is Hercules." She spoke softly, wanting both to get his attention and to recall his humanity. "Long ago, before you were born, Hercules promised to be my friend and yours." She waited for a response from him, and when it seemed to her that he was able to focus on her face, she said, "These are my children, Hercules. Medeius, my eldest; Argus; and my daughter Eriopus."

He gave no sign of hearing. In the silence, the first of the summer's cicadas began its harsh, metallic whir, and she jumped at the noise. The cicada's hum flared and died three times, and she grew more and more uneasy. Then, with his free hand, Hercules slowly pushed the helmet back, and his eyes seemed to come alive. In the manner of a man who hadn't spoken for so long that he'd almost forgotten how, he cleared his throat and said, "The boys . . . are like you. The girl . . . him. Blonde. Soft."

"For all that, they are themselves," she said pleasantly, when it appeared he'd lost his train of thought again.

"And you? Are you yourself?" He was staring at the children now, and they seemed almost petrified with fright. "Do Jason and his children make you happy?"

"Who is Hercules to ask if I am happy?" His question suddenly angered her. "Look at yourself, a prince of Thebes, wandering as if you have no home. Dusty. Dirty. Come back with us and rest. Let me heal you."

"No!" The cry was as much warning as refusal. He looked directly at her for the first time. "No," he repeated more gently. "Keep away from me. There are things I must do . . . things I think I've done. . . ."

"Surely you can rest? Jason is away, but we can care for you. Allow us at least to give you meat and wine?"

"You don't need my help?"

"I always need a friend."

"You will need *Hercules* . . . and all that he is. . . ." He half turned from her and added, "and Hercules will need Medea. I don't know when, but I can feel it coming." His mad eyes shifted again to the children. "You should control him now. Stop time. Before he shames you. You have the power, Medea. You have always had the power. If you don't use it, who will heal you then?"

"Jason is as he always was," she said gently, meaning that she loved him.

"Yes," he agreed. "And you have never truly seen him. As if you are yourself bewitched. But you will. Unless you make him fear you now. I made him fear me."

He glanced away and fell silent, then suddenly began walking, as if he'd forgotten all about them. But when he drew even with the children at the bottom of the slope, he paused again and frowned. "If the gods were kind," he said, "one of you would rule Corinth, and one Colchis, and one Iolcus. That was the future your mother planned for you. Never trust the gods to be kind."

He left them then with no farewell and no backward look.

THIRTEEN

AN AUTUMN CAME WHEN JASON SENT MEDEIUS away to live among the centaurs, the horsetribes on Mt. Pelion's slopes, where he would be schooled by their leader, Chiron, and trained as a warrior, as his father was before him. Medea felt it was the boy's absence that made that winter seem especially bleak.

Bitter cold and snowy though it was, the winter caused no great hardship; there was food and fuel enough for everyone. While most appreciated the novelty of being able to rest from field work, the garrison, the warriors, and particularly the king, were bored. There were no border wars to fight, no need to hunt, and too much snow for visitors. Wrestling, games, and wine grew tiresome.

It was snowing the morning Jason went away. He was going to ride to Mt. Pelion, he said. "To see our son and visit Chiron. I may return by way of Thebes and visit Hercules—for old times' sake. I don't know how long I'll be gone." He avoided meeting her eyes as he spoke.

"To ride so far in the snow?" she said, worried. "Why not go by ship?"

"The ride will do me good. I'm getting soft."

She watched him go and felt great unease. He took half the garrison with him and many of the slaves. Weeks passed with no word from him. Snow became rain, and her unease became worry. No sooner had the melting snow made travel possible than a merchant arrived from Thebes. She sent for him, and to her great relief, he told her that "King Jason spent half the winter in Thebes. He's still there. I saw him myself, living in the palace like a son, they say."

She was so relieved it didn't even bother her sense of pride to think that now a lowly merchant knew that Jason hadn't bothered to write.

Two days later a message finally arrived from Jason: "Jason, king of Corinth, gives you leave to prepare a feast to celebrate his return to Corinth," the runner recited. "He will arrive in five days' time."

Beacon fires told of his coming when he was still two days away. He returned not on Bunus's old roan, but riding a fine black stallion, the gift of King Creon of Thebes. He was dressed as he had been the first time she saw him, in a leather tunic and leopard skin, but both these garments were new. He'd lost weight and hennaed his hair and beard and looked younger.

With him rode a company of Theban nobles. These men barely acknowledged her greeting but stared openly at her. In their presence Jason seemed strange and withdrawn. Had she been younger, the Thebans' attitude would have enraged her, but by now she was familiar with Greek manners—especially where women were concerned. She rationalized their rudeness as provincialism, but Jason's coolness puzzled her—when she had time to think in the confusion of making comfortable so many unexpected guests, as well as finding quarters for their horses and slaves.

"You haven't told me how Medeius is," she said when she and Jason accidentally found themselves alone together for a moment in midafternoon.

"Not learning as fast as he could."

"And your foster father, Chiron, is he well?"

"Getting older." As he spoke, his glance flicked over the hall. "You've had it painted again, I see. You must have known we were coming."

"And Hercules?"

"There was no time to visit him," he said and walked away.

He's gone nowhere near Mt. Pelion, she thought, watching him go. He's not seen Chiron or Medeius. Why is he lying to me?

The feast was held outdoors so that all the city might share in the celebration. The day was fine and sunny. Rows of trestle tables held trays of delicacies, meats, fruit, and bread. Further down the slope, aromatic smoke and steam rose from the pit where all varieties of meats, fowl, and fish were baking. There was heavy traffic between the tables, the cooking pit, and the terrace where the wine was being poured. There were games and music grand enough to impress any guest.

Oddly enough, Jason seemed to disapprove, even though he had requested the feast. "Excess!" was his comment when he joined her at their table beneath the royal canopy. "You are always compelled to behave with excess."

"Unlike yourself. Your reputation is based solely on modesty and a shy demeanor," she said with a laugh. To her relief, he laughed, too, his ill humor apparently gone as fast as it had come. He ate and drank with every appearance of enjoyment. The guests' first rush to appease their hunger left the couple rare minutes of privacy.

"Do you remember the first feast we shared?" As Jason spoke, he watched a flock of cranes flying in the distance. Silhouetted against the orange cloud in the west, their elegant black forms suggested animated hieroglyphics.

"At the Dawn Palace." Her voice was soft with memory. "You didn't like the lettuce. You still don't."

"Did you love me even then?"

"I loved you from the first moment I saw you."

He smiled, as if pleased by her admission, then, still smiling, said: "The gods made you love me, Medea. Because you served their purpose, and my own. I felt nothing for you. I never have. I married you only because of a sense of honor. You remain what you were then, a barbarian princess, half Greek at best, with the haggling spirit of a wine merchant." His tone was quietly conversational, as if he were expressing a mild distaste for barley bread. He kept his gaze fixed on the western sky.

Below them on the small arena stage, wrestlers engaged in bawdy antics to amuse the guests. It was to the sound of ribald Greek laughter that Medea finally allowed herself to understand. Her feet and hands went

[*184*]

cold. Bitter bile rose in her throat. She swallowed carefully to avoid choking.

A golden light reflecting from the clouds lit his face and hair with kindness, washing out the graying strands, erasing lines around his eyes and those small furrows of discontent not hidden by his beard. That familiar profile, so beloved, so deceitful . . . in all these years she'd never seen his chin. As he spoke, he was nervously turning the ram's-head ring on his right forefinger, a ring she had given him years ago.

"Surely ten years of my life are payment enough for the Sacred Fleece?" He leaned closer, glancing at her for a reaction. "Besides, when all is said and done, my getting the Fleece gained me nothing, did it? Thanks to the evil way in which you killed Pelias, I lost Iolcus. Half of the Argonauts are no longer my friends. Ten years is more than enough payment for that. Don't you agree?" Before she could say anything, he went on, "In fact, I've decided that it is you who are indebted to me. If it weren't for me, you would never have been queen of Corinth. You never would have come to Greece. To settle your debt, I'm going to divorce you, and you are going to give me Corinth—as a wedding gift."

He dared to meet her eyes then, to see if he had shocked her, as he obviously intended to do. "I'm going to marry Glauce, the daughter of King Creon of Thebes. Our two cities will form an alliance."

She felt as if the earth had disappeared beneath her, and she floated alone, disembodied, an entity composed of rage and grief and sharp physical pain. He had never loved her. Never. She had been a pawn. Duped. Something for him to use.

"Silence?" His half whisper was mocking, goading. "Don't tell me you've become a good Greek woman at last?"

Killing him would be so easy, a matter of reaching out and touching that vulnerable spot on his neck, there, where his hair curled so invitingly. Or she could will him to stand up and fall on his sword, or tear out both his eyes. He wanted to divorce her, to marry another woman, to bring that woman here, to the palace she had rebuilt? To give another woman all that she had, out of love, given to him?

"Corinth is mine." Her effort to control her rage made her voice low and sure. "It was my father's land, as you recall, and it will be my son's. You are its king only because of your marriage to me. If you divorce me, you lose all claim to it."

"No." He was very sure of himself. "The Corinthians have no respect for you. I've seen to that. They don't remember your father. So far as they are concerned, a non-Greek woman is not a wife—only a possession. If you kill me, they will rebel against you, unless you kill them all. If you try to dispose of me by force, you'll find the garrison will obey me, not you. And if they're told how you killed Corinthus, to say nothing of Pelias—"

"Those things were done for you!"

He smiled with satisfaction at finally rousing her anger and blithely went on. ". . . and of course I would have to tell them. You shouldn't confess things in moments of intimacy if you don't want the secret to come back to haunt you later. And think of the future, Medea. Your son could never rule. The Corinthians will never

[*186*]

accept as their king the son of a barbarian witch, a known poisoner. And for all your talents, you are quite mortal. You, too, can be killed. But if you leave quietly, because I'm not completely ungrateful to you, I'll let you take your brats with you into exile."

He was deliberately trying to goad her into unthinking rage, she realized then, hoping she would attack him. Which explained why there were several Thebans standing too close to the royal table; they were waiting to "protect" Jason.

What he said was true. Because she had allowed it, encouraged it, the Corinthian people did attribute their new prosperity to Jason, while she, after all this time, was seen, at best, as his barbarian queen. Now he threatened her and her children with death.

Hercules' prediction had come true; this was Jason as he truly was. Atalanta had once told her to never trust a man's sacred oath until she knew what he hoped to gain by swearing.

"Do you remember the sacred oath you once swore to all your gods?" she asked him then. "You swore to keep faith with me forever."

"That was under coercion!" A lull in the crowd noise made his indignant cry carry. Guests turned to stare. Jason waved and smiled, then leaned over and whispered in her ear. "Oaths sworn under the threat of death are invalid. The gods know that. You should, too, if you're as learned as you claim."

Now she knew what he hoped to gain—everything. She was to lose him, lose Corinth, lose her home, lose all her dreams. In return, he would give her and her children humiliation, scorn, and poverty. For him she had betrayed her father, seen her half brother butchered, and been responsible for the deaths of two men who were, she now saw, no worse than Jason. And she had alienated Circe.

She had been sad when he'd sent Medeius to Mt. Pelion; now she hoped the boy's being there might save his life—for if Jason claimed the throne, he would let no rightful heir live, especially since he planned to remarry. Perhaps he had already gone to Mt. Pelion and killed her son? At that thought, cold rage overcame her. She reached for the small dagger always concealed in the folds of her gown—then paused. The royal bodyguards were watching her closely. He had chosen this time and place to tell her, thought the whole thing out carefully. The guards were not there simply to protect him—but to kill her! If in anger she attacked him, he could have her killed in full view of the guests—and claim self-defense. There was no one here in Corinth or anywhere else who would dare to dispute his claim. Or wish to. And then all her children would surely die.

The Goddess sometimes waited a long time to make her punishments effective.

When the queen abruptly rose and left the royal table, her husband's Theban guests smiled to themselves. The other guests paid no attention—the wrestlers had added an unmuzzled bear to their act. The servants, with their instinct for self-preservation, faded into the shadows as Medea passed by.

Entering the palace, she grabbed a torch from its wall socket, oblivious to the weight or the sparks that fell on her bare arms and shoulders. When she entered her workroom, the slam of the massive door echoed through the wing.

Anyone who had seen her frenzy of activity that night would have been sure both that she was a sorceress and that she had gone mad. Her face was gray, her eyes owl-wide, and she talked to herself constantly as she worked, an angry muttering that went on and on in the monotone of shock.

As if she couldn't get heat enough or light, she lit every lamp, built fires in the hearth, the kiln, and the furnace in the courtyard. Still wearing all of her jewelry and her finest gown, she searched through her stores, collecting charcoal, white sand, alkaline salts, old bones, and coal. She brought out Circe's carved black chest, from it took a small glass disk and weighed it in her hand. The glass could focus the rays of the sun, burn skin, set straw ablaze. She stared at it a long time.

After stirring the charcoal in the furnace, she increased the heat, then carefully measured the sand and alkali into a heavy vessel. While the glass was cooking, she hunted through her shelves for molds. By dawn, three large magnifying glasses and thirty half spheres, each the size of her thumbnail, were cooling in their molds.

She returned to her apartment, removed her ruined finery, bathed, dressed and ate. Her serving women might have been stone for all the attention she gave them. It was her habit to visit the children each morning. She did so now. If her disgrace was already public knowledge, she did not want it said that she was hiding out of fear or humiliation.

Guards followed her. More guards lounged outside

the children's rooms. Jason was taking no chance of her spiriting the children to safety, thus depriving him of hostages to control her, should he need to. Assured the children were safe and well, she returned to the court-yard of her workroom. She was calmer now, her rage more deadly.

Into the lower vessel of her vacuum chamber she loaded measured quantities of sand, coal, and phospho-rescent bones. The three large magnifying glasses were positioned on a frame above the furnace, their rays focused on the cooking chamber to increase the tem-perature. Into the vacuum jar went the small half spheres of glass, their rounded sides buried in wet sand; strips of heavy linen; and a quantity of gauze. The container was clamped and sealed, the air pumped out. The sun was bright and the fire hot. Soon a chemical odor began to permeate the courtyard. For safety she went inside the workroom and shut the door.

Late that night, when the furnace was cold, she opened the vacuum chamber. The interior glowed like a snowfield. Using tongs, she carefully removed the cloth from the vacuum jar and slid it into an oiled sharkskin; then lifted out the half spheres of glass and daubed wax on the base of each, sealing in a blister of white phosphorus. She made sure none of the glowing stuff touched her skin or clothing. Carefully, too, all the excess phosphorus was put into a covered jar of water and the jar buried in a corner of the courtyard. The white-coated glass and cloth were sealed into caches in the workroom walls.

When everything had been put away and all trace of her work cleaned up, she stood for a time staring at the lamplight flickering over the uneven surface of the wall.

"Only the stones will remain!" she whispered to the silence. "Only the stones!" And then the queen of Corinth fainted into a sleep of exhaustion on the dirt floor.

The robe was made so full and fine that each fold draped and fell in soft, perfect lines. The half rounds glowed like pearls. Radiating out from each pearl were delicate needles of a silvery substance—metallic sodium from the deserts of Libya, formed when lightning struck certain salt pans. Medea herself put on the decorations, handling them with tweezers, knotting with gold wire. When she was done, the robe was all and more than she wanted it to be, a thing of great beauty that glistened like starlight on snow. From her jewels she chose a thin crownlet of gold and lined it also with the silvery stuff, and her gift was complete.

She resumed her normal routine, as much as she could. Jason had her and the children watched and followed wherever they went. She met him once, by accident, as he left the stable one morning. The contempt on his face when he looked at her added to her anger.

"Keep away from me."

"I intend to," she said. "Have you noticed, Jason, that for the first time the people here seem to like me? Not for anything I've done to improve their lives, but because they know you're sending me and the children into exile. And they can *pity* me." She smiled at him then, a smile he never forgot. "You've made me an object of pity. I'll never forgive you for that."

It was true.

"The shame of him!" her twelve slave girls complained to other wives. "He'd have no kingdom without her—nothing—yet he says she can take away with her only what she was carrying when she first entered the palace. We were her wedding gift from Queen Arete. She was always good to us. And we're to be taken from her, along with all our children! If he's so greedy with the queen, how greedy will he be at tax time? Especially when she goes?"

At first their talk was dismissed as the whimperings of favorites out of luck, but—considering who they were—what they said had gossip value and was repeated. People grudgingly admitted that, while the queen was a barbarian, she met adversity with dignity. Where most women would have raged and wept, she was calm and dry-eyed; she even had the palace prepared for the wedding feast.

The floor of the hall was scoured and waxed. Oil, wine, and honey were brought in and stored in the anteroom cisterns as a display of Jason's wealth. She had the fountain drained and cleaned; the servants saw her late that night carefully installing strips of glowing white fabric around the fountain's edge. "So that the water will look more inviting," she explained softly. Water lilies were floated in the pool, along with a small tubbed cedar. When the morning sun lit the water and sent light shimmering over the walls, all agreed that the hall had never been more beautiful, or looked so fit for a wedding.

When the beacon fires signaled the approach of King Creon and his daughter, Jason led the procession that went to meet the Theban's ship. He drove the chariot and team that Medea had given him. He was followed by all the nobles of Corinth and Thebes, the council, and the garrison. Musicians accompanied him, creating glad noise, and garlanded girls walked with baskets, strewing flowers and fresh thyme. Corinth's welcome for Jason's second bride was far different than that for his first. Medea was confined to her apartment with orders to be gone before sunset of the next day—Jason's wedding day.

The shrill of flutes and drums drew her to the window as the procession returned to the palace. The first thing she saw was Princess Glauce riding beside Jason in the place that had always been Medea's. Behind Glauce stood Creon, like a tall, stern post. Jason was dressed in pale blue, embroidered with fringes of gold the color of his hair. The Theban girl was tall, with bushy blonde hair, from which the tails of a green ribbon fluttered in the wind. So far as beauty went, youth was her greatest asset. Watching, Medea remembered her own wedding in the cave, the secrecy, the dust, the Fleece draped on the wedding couch. Yes, Jason deserved what she planned for him. And more.

The next day, when the guests had all assembled in the hall and the festivities had begun, Medea's sons, Argus and Alcimedes—who was five years old and her baby—entered the great room. They carried between them a large brass tray with handles. The robe lay on the tray. Atop the folds of precious silk, like sunset on a snowy peak, lay the delicate gold crown with its silvery lining.

Curiosity made the guests step back and open an avenue so that all could see the children as they entered. Dressed as warrior princes, complete with shining brass greaves, breastplates and pleated white leather skirts, they were a sight to make any parent proud. Their physical beauty, combined with the obvious richness of the gift, drew cries of admiration.

Seeing them come, Jason moved to intercept them, but the crowd of people, some of whom had already had too much to drink, slowed his progress across the room until it was too late to stop them without appearing boorish—and afraid of their mother.

"Glauce, daughter of Creon, most noble princess of Thebes," Argus recited as they stopped in front of her, "the sons of Jason beg you to accept this gift to welcome you to Corinth." The boy smiled up at her, as if relieved to have remembered the words his royal mother had made him memorize.

Glauce smiled, too, not at Argus or his little brother, but at the gift they carried. She reached for the crown like a greedy child, weighed it with both hands, smiled more broadly and put it on her head, pushing it down over the tangle of her curls. She picked up the robe and swirled it over her shoulders like a cape, letting the elegant fabric settle down and envelop her. She looked, if not regal, at least much improved by the lovely garment.

The crowd responded with a chorus of appreciative *ahhs* as Glauce looked to her father, Creon, for his approval, then turned to find Jason, obviously assuming he was her benefactor.

The two little boys set down the tray and hurried from the hall. Jason caught the gleam of their black hair as they stepped off the porch into the sunshine in the courtyard. He hurried to the window and was just about to call out to a guard to stop them and bring them back when a guest shouted: "A toast to King

Jason and his excellent taste in women's clothing!" Everyone laughed, and a golden drinking cup was placed in his hand. "A toast to his taste in women!" a Theban noble called, and there was more laughter.

The wedding guests milled about, drinking, eating, jostling one another, pressing close to see the robe. In their midst, Glauce and her father were eagerly examining this unexpected treasure; while the crown's value was obvious, neither had ever seen silk or such elaborate decoration. They were none too subtle in their attempts to establish the worth of the fabric.

The afternoon was warm. Sunlight slanted across Glauce's head and shoulders. Her body heat and perspiration were softening the wax seals on the half spheres filled with white phosphorus. When she traced a star ray with her finger, trying to feel the metal's weight, the sweat on her hands excited the unstable metal. A small blue flame flashed up the strip, melting the wax and igniting the phosphorus inside. At the same time, sweat trickled down beneath her hair and touched the rim of the crown, and its silver lining ignited.

Robe and crown flashed into flames so quick and hot that she had breath enough for only one scream of pain and terror before she whirled and threw herself full length into the fountain. The resulting splash lowered the pool's water level, exposing to the air the phosphorous-impregnated strips of linen lining the rim. As soon as water struck the crown, there was an explosive roar. The very water burned; flames shot up to the ceiling and out the smoke hole. The metallic sodium, in its contact with the water, seemed to remember the lightning that had created it so long ago in the desert.

Those guests fortunate enough to be in the court-yard caught a glimpse of a human torch burning with blue white incandescence, her robe shooting sparks the length and width of the hall. They could scream be-cause they were outside; the guests inside had neither time enough nor oxygen to express their horror or their agony.

Jason, still near the window, heard Glauce's death cry. With his animal instinct for self-preservation, he wasted no time in trying to see what could be wrong. He knocked aside two guests as he leaped to safety and was clear of the porch and running as the hall exploded into flames.

Within minutes, the cistern of stored olive oil ig-nited. Roof and wall timbers began to burn beneath the plaster. Soon the very stones were hot enough to crack.

Hearing the shouts and then screams, Medea went to her window. Flames were torching up around the oblong slab of roof covering the smoke hole of the hall. From their knobby mud nests under the eaves, the swallows were fleeing, darting up, swooping out across the hill, abandoning their nestlings in their fright. That one detail told her all she needed to know.

Servants sympathetic to her had promised to have the children ready, the horses waiting. With chilling calm, she picked up a leather bag much like the one she had first carried to Corinth and, without a backward glance, left the rooms she'd lived in for a decade. There were no guards about.

Oily black smoke swirled around the building, the heat of the fire creating its own deadly wind. Flames were licking up the wooden pillars of the gallery. In the courtyard a fire brigade had formed, but water only spread the flames. People were running and shouting, some attempting to help others, some already looting. In the stables the horses screamed and plunged and frantically kicked their stalls.

As she hurried across the outer gallery, she saw that the door to the children's apartment stood ajar. Something red had been spilled on the floor. The heavy smell of fresh blood reached her then, and, with sudden, sickening insight, she knew what she would find. Jason had meant exactly what he said: "You will leave Corinth with only those things you brought with you." She had not had the children then. Her legs wanted to buckle. She willed them to carry her.

Blonde Eriopus lay half covered by the body of her nurse; the same sword slash had killed them both. Beside them, still in their warrior finery, were the bodies of Argus and Alcimedes. They had been beheaded.

With a pitiful moan, she sank to her knees and caught up each small, still body, hugging them close, as if she could will them back to life. Their blood soaked her and all she wore. "Why this?" she shouted to the Goddess. "Why my babies? Why kill them to punish me? Why—" And then her glance lit on a pair of bloody palm prints on the floor—made by someone who had knelt to lick the blood. *To keep the ghost from haunting me.* She could see Jason doing this, see him killing his own children as easily as he had killed Apsyrtus.

Her screams of loss and grief and rage cut through all the noise below, but no one seemed to hear her, or if they did, paid no attention. Her own acts of bitter vengeance had been too well planned. Her fire was consuming all the feeling left in Corinth.

FOURTEEN

SPRING WAS ALL AROUND HER, fresh and green. She saw none of it. She stopped only when the mare was tired. While the horse grazed or slept, she sat and stared, benumbed. She felt nothing, not hunger, thirst, cold or pain, and was unaware of people. Those few who saw her quickly hid, frightened by her appearance. She was smeared with old blood and what they assumed to be the greasy ashes of a burnt sacrifice. She wore a gown, a rag now, and a gold crown and breast piece inlaid with precious stones, bracelets on both arms and ankles—and for all this display of wealth, no man dared to rob her.

On the third day out, she had stopped to let the mare drink and was sitting under an ancient olive tree covered with tiny, creamy flowers. Near her left hand a small tortoise walked on claw tips, unsure if the bulk it perceived as her was dangerous. Movement on the rocks below attracted her attention. Three fluffy wolf cubs had come out of their den to play. As she watched, one of the pups, still a clumsy infant, tumbled down the little hill. Its two brothers joyously bounded after—*like the children playing on the hill the day we saw Hercules.*

At the image, pain cut through the numbness and bent her double, drawing her lips back to expose her teeth in agony. She twisted over, and her fists pounded the stone in helpless frustration. She wanted her children, and they were gone, forever beyond her embrace. Her first strangled sob scared the tortoise into its shell, and the wolf cubs fled. She cried until there were no more tears to cry and then shook with dry sobs. By sunset her eyes and mouth were parched. Shaking with exhaustion, she crawled to the stream bank and drank by cupping water in her hand. The cold liquid revived her a little and eased her pain by numbing. For the first time she noticed her knuckles were raw and bleeding but didn't know how that had happened. When she'd rested a bit, she eased herself down into the water and washed herself, giving the remains of her gown to the current.

As she watched the rag being rushed downstream and sunk beneath the foamy rapids, it occurred to her how easy it would be to move out into the swift current and let the water take her, too. She was alone. Forever. All she had once had or wanted or loved was lost. Irrevocably gone. She had no place to go and no place she wanted to go. She could seek asylum with Hercules—who was not only half mad but married to Creon's oldest daughter, Glauce's sister. Once she would have smiled at the complete irony of such a situation; now it wasn't worth the bother.

A hawk cried overhead. As she looked up, she slipped and fell onto her back in the cushioning water.

The current rushed her downstream, spun her sideways and nudged her onto a gravel bar with such force that her knees were skinned. Like a puppet, she jerked to her feet and walked up the bank to her mare. There, almost of their own will, her arms reached up to remove the gold she wore and put it in her leather bag. From the pannier she removed and donned a deerskin tunic and a long cloak for warmth, and found cheese, bread and wine, which she consumed, although she felt no hunger. That done, she had the strength to lift the pannier from the mare and hobble her to graze. Using the wicker basket as a windscreen, she curled up in the shelter of a hollow beech and fell into a dead sleep that lasted until long past dawn.

She dreamed she was a child again in the Temple of the Goddess and Circe was there, robed in green as lush and rich as spring. "Your children are safe now," Circe said to her. "Their souls have been made stars and placed in the night sky to shine forever in pure, white innocence. They have no memory of you or of their father. Or of what the two of you have done.

"Jason escaped your fire—and murdered your children. Because the gods admire your spirit, they regret the trick they played on you—making you love Jason without thought, making you half mad in your obsession. You are made immortal, their attempt to compensate you for the grief their meddling caused you. Jason they have made an exile; for the rest of his life he is condemned to wander from city to city, homeless, a beggar, despised by gods and mortals. The time will come when he will wish that he had died quickly in the fire you prepared for him. For the gods heard the oath he swore to you—of his own free will—in all their

[*201*]

names that night. They will exact vengeance for his betrayal."

"I don't want to be immortal," Medea cried, "to hurt
like this forever. I don't want my poor babies to be
stars, isolate and cold. I want the earth. I want what
used to be!"

But Circe was gone.

Hercules' palace stood alone on a hill outside
Thebes, surrounded by a cypress grove so old and dark
and gloomy that no birds sang there. As Medea approached, she frowned to see that all the shutters were
closed. The track she rode was weed-choked and rutted, the fields and vineyards untended, although grain
and grapes were growing. Goats grazed without a shepherd, and most had lost their precious long wool to
thorns. There was no guard at the entrance, not even
so much as a goose. She dismounted and led the mare
up to the portico.

"Hello?" she called. "Is anyone here?"

In the quiet a raven could be heard complaining on
a distant oak. The massive door to the hall stood half
open, windswept leaves against its base. Puzzled, she
tied the mare to a bush and cautiously walked into the
gloom.

"Hercules?"

His name echoed in the dimness. There were faint,
scratchy noises, as if small animals were scurrying into
hiding. The hall was empty. Light from the smoke hole
showed old ashes in the hearth. Bats hung from the
roof beams like leather plums.

The rooms leading from the hall were huge, cavelike
chambers, damp and dark, where her solitary footsteps

echoed. The furniture was sparse and broken, the wall hangings ripped to pieces. Without warning, a servant appeared, sidling out of a dark passage, her back against the wall, as if she expected attack. At the sight of Medea she stopped short, screamed and fled.

Medea no longer cared enough about anything to be frightened, but she was puzzled by the woman's reaction. After a moment's hesitation, she ran after her, calling, "Wait! Come back here!" but the woman was gone. Coming to an open stairs, Medea climbed the steps, carefully picking her way over litter. The rooms on the second floor were as dark and empty as those below.

Tired now and wanting fresh air and light, she climbed on up to the roof. From there she could have seen the rooftops and temples of Thebes, had she bothered to look. Next to the steps was a stone bench, and she sat down to rest. Plainly, she had come to the wrong place. Perhaps Hercules had built another, newer home within view of this one?

As she stood up to see, down at the far end of the roof, half hidden by an overhanging cypress, a large animal moved. She caught only a glimpse of fur before the thing disappeared behind a dividing wall. Her first instinct was to ignore it; whatever it was, it was welcome to this ruin for a lair. But then she thought of the possible danger to her horse, drew her dagger, and crept closer to investigate.

It was Hercules. He sat naked and hunched up, his huge arms hugging his knees so tightly that his muscles bulged and strained. His eyes were wide and unfocused; his jaws clenched, his throat working. As she watched, appalled, he began to rock in that spastic frenzy peculiar to lunatics. Faster and faster he rocked, until his heels were lifting higher with each backward lunge, and he finally tipped over and fell sideways, his head thudding against the roof. Unfazed, his arms still locked around his knees, he tried to continue rocking.

Giving no sign that he was aware of her, or of the fact that the roof's rough surface had scraped his right arm raw from elbow to shoulder, he stopped as abruptly as he'd begun, stretched out, rolled onto his back and stared up at the glare of milky sky. There were sores all over him, some scabbed, some wet and seeping. Flies buzzed around him. Sandals, sword belt, and the lion pelt and skull had all worn bald spots in his body hair. That he had neither bathed nor left this section of roof for some time was plain from the filth around and on him.

"Do you see it?"

She jumped, startled by the unexpectedness of the question as well as by his tone of voice. He sounded like an excited child enthused by something.

"Do you see it?" He flung his arm up, forefinger pointing at the sky. She looked, and high overhead saw a vulture circling, waiting. Above the first, two more circled. "Nobody likes them but me," said Hercules. "They fly with more majesty and grace than any hawk or eagle. They are big and strong! The mightiest birds I've ever seen! Their beaks and talons could rip out the living heart of any man or child or sheep. But they never do. They never do. They only eat what death leaves. They never take a life. Never tear living flesh." He giggled childishly, then instantly became sad. "But no one appreciates their nobility. They have a sacred mission to keep the earth free from corruption. Why doesn't anyone appreciate them, Mother?"

Before she could think of an answer, Hercules went on. "I was born to save gods and man from corruption. So my true father told you. So you in turn told me. Always. Your husband tried to kill me. To save the nurse's milk for my brother. He called my brother his heir . . . as if I were a cuckoo in the nest. But it was me who strangled the vipers while my mortal twin screamed in terror. I don't know why he screamed; the snakes were in my bed. The king had put them there. . . ."

The little-boy voice trailed off. He had been distracted by the sight of blood trickling down his arm. As he watched it, his face twisted with grief and he began to cry. "I'm not like that. I'm good. I've always been a gentle boy." He rolled over onto his stomach, hid his head in his arms and sobbed, as if brokenhearted. She found her own eyes filling in response.

She reached out quickly to put him into deep sleep, but even in madness his responses were fast. Her fingers had barely touched his neck when, with a growl, he twisted back on her, the little boy gone, the animal returned. Impeded by his mop of hair, her fingers missed the mark; only by clutching his throat and desperately hanging on as he rolled back to crush her did she succeed in knocking him out. His body went limp; his upper torso fell like a dead weight on top of her, his filthy hair a smelly mass hanging in her face. She escaped by pushing his head sideways, allowing its great weight to lift his left shoulder far enough for her to inch free.

Bruised and panting from fear and exhaustion, she lay still for a moment in the sun, then heard whispering and sat up. The servant woman and two men stood watching her from a safe distance. Behind them were more than a dozen other slaves.

"Are you a ghost? Or a goddess come to claim him?" asked a man.

"Neither. A friend."

"You killed him?" the woman dared to ask in her odd Theban accent. Her awed whisper suggested Hercules' death was something both desirable and inevitable.

"He's asleep."

"He looks dead."

"You can't kill an immortal," the other man told the woman.

"Bring a litter," Medea ordered. "We must carry him to his rooms. He won't waken," she assured them as they began to back away in fear. After some verbal bullying, they obeyed, although it was plain they were terrified of him and herself as well. Who but a witch could have calmed his rage to sleep?

It took six men to lift him. When he was stretched out on his couch, she drugged him so that he would sleep for days, and then had him bathed and his hair washed. When he was clean and dry, she dressed his wounds and covered him for warmth.

He had been mad, the slaves told her, ever since the Euboean sneak attack on Thebes. At the head of the Theban forces, Hercules had defeated the attackers and taken their king captive. As punishment, he had had the man tied to chariots and torn apart, then refused to let the pieces be buried. The gods, said the slaves, were disgusted by his brutality, which grew worse each year, and they had driven him mad as punishment.

He had come home raving mad, and the first thing he had seen was his sons practicing martial arts in the courtyard with their tutor. Shouting "No son of mine will ever go to war! I'll spare them that horror!" he had clubbed to death both boys and their tutors. Then he went to his wife's rooms and killed her to keep her from ever learning how her sons had died.

Since that awful day, he had either mourned or raved, attacking anyone he saw. King Creon had sent eighty soldiers to take him prisoner. Hercules killed them all. In desperation, four of his serving men had tried to trap him with a heavy net. He clubbed them to death. He had no need to eat or drink and slept only fitfully. No one else dared to approach him. What remained of the household staff had gone into hiding, and many had since run away.

"No one from Thebes has come near this place since the snows last winter," the slave woman said. "Not since King Creon announced that Hercules and his family had gone away on a long journey."

"Did Jason of Corinth come here?"

"No." The name seemed to mean nothing to them. "You are the first."

At her orders, they barred his door, not that the bars would hold him for long, but if he battered his way out, the noise would give the household warning. They took everything out of the room but his marble sleeping couch and the stone window bench, where Medea sometimes sat to watch over him as he slept.

She restored order to his palace. She wanted him to heal and be well, and there was no healing solace in the chaos of this place. The shutters were opened to let in light and air; the rooms where murder had been done were scrubbed and purified with fire, sweet-smelling herbs, and rushes. The courtyard, too, was purified and a day of mourning observed with sacrifices and a funeral feast.

While his slaves were uneasy in her presence, they welcomed her control over him. A few who had run away returned, now that there was food to be had. Some of the herds and flocks were found, the spring newborn counted; work began again in the vineyards, orchards, and fields. Life quickly assumed an almost normal tenor. But all of them, including Medea, kept alert for any sound from Hercules' room.

His sleep, like his illness, was unnatural. Even with the drugs, he slept too long. She watched over him, going in at intervals throughout the day, sitting with him at night. He did not move for days; only the faint misting of a mirror held to his nose proved he was still breathing. One sunset he sighed, turned to face the rosy light and entered into more normal rest. The night he finally woke, she was sitting by the window.

"Who are you?"

His husky whisper roused her from an exhausted doze. For a moment she thought she'd been wakened by the cicadas in the trees outside; then she saw him move. He reached down and picked up the water pitcher from the floor by the bed, drank with some difficulty and lay back exhausted.

"Who are you?" he asked again, his whisper stronger now.

"Medea."

He stared at her as an infant or a hunting animal

stares, eyes wide and round, reflecting only points of lamplight. "Do I know you?"

"Yes."

"Who am I?"

"Some call you Hercules."

At the mention of this name, his eyes shut, as if he felt pain. "Who is Hercules? Why do they call me that name?"

"You don't remember?"

He shook his head.

"Then I shall tell you about him. You rest and listen. You've been very ill and are still weak."

"Yes," he agreed, and opened his eyes again.

As he continued to stare at her, she leaned back against the window casement and clasped her hands around one knee, as if relaxed. "Of all the men in Greece," she began, "Hercules was the finest. His mother said he was the son of Zeus and not her husband's child. She was Alcmene, queen of Thebes, wife of King Amphitryon. She made sure her favorite son had the finest tutors so that he might excel as a warrior, horseman, musician, and scholar. He was a gentle boy, as kind to animals and slaves as he was to nobles. He was as strong as he was gifted, but he never abused that strength . . . well, only once. When he was ten years old, a substitute music tutor beat him for playing in the manner his regular teacher had taught him to play. Because the punishment was so unjust, the boy lost his temper and hit the man with his lyre—killing him with one blow.

"As punishment, Hercules was sent away to live among the tribes who tended the royal Theban cattle." She paused to make sure he was still awake, and he motioned for her to continue. "The boy was happy there. In the starry uplands, he learned astronomy from a retired freedman and philosophy from a lonely Athenian exile, but as time passed, he grew restless. At eighteen he sailed with an amber merchant, north to Hyperborea. He visited the great island where the tin mines are and where men paint themselves blue. He saw lands of endless snow and tribes who herded deer, which they harnessed to sleds and drove like horses. This Hercules told to friends, and friends told to me."

Like that of an absorbed child, Hercules' gaze never left her face. When she stopped again to think, he prompted her with: "What happened next?"

"That depends on who tells his story. Hercules had many great adventures. I know only a few of the stories."

"Tell me all you know? Please?" he begged.

It seemed to both of them then that time mercifully stopped as she told him the tales she had once told her own children, and for a little while she was almost happy again, forgetting the past was gone. Hercules listened enthralled until she reached the present and told him what had happened to Hercules' wife and sons and household. At that, he began to move restlessly and sat up, hugging his knees and rocking, watching her as if it were vital to keep the reality of her firmly in his mind.

". . . but if the gods caused his madness, then they did so long ago, for he was mad when we first met ten years past."

"You think the gods are innocent?"

"No. But neither is Hercules. The gods made him—made *you*—unique. No matter how far you traveled, you never found an equal. For all of the suppliants, admirers, and rivals—you have no true friend. For all of your lovers, no one you truly love. As your awareness of your loneliness grows, so does your desperation at your inability to change what cannot be changed. And then to know you are immortal . . ."

She leaned toward him and took his huge hands in hers, hoping touch would bring him more into reality. "When we met, Hercules, you offered me friendship and understanding. You knew I was mad then with passion for Jason. I've since become familiar with the violence born of rage. I can understand you more than I could have then. I have the knowledge to heal you, physically, and to be your friend, but I cannot change what you've done, or what you are. No more than I can change what I am, or my past. Perhaps no more than you can help me."

His eyes searched her face, as if he were pleading with her to deny what she'd just said. When she did not, he looked away, past her, to memory. His head sank and he groaned with pain. As a sob escaped, he twisted away to hide his face. "I killed them! I am Hercules and before all the gods, I killed my own family!"

His roar of grief frightened awake every person in the palace, and every animal on the hillside hushed to hear his terrible weeping. She didn't try to comfort him, knowing he was beyond comfort. When his sobs finally subsided into noisy hiccups, she poured him a mug of wine. "Drink this," she said. He obeyed without hesitation and also ate the barley bread and cheese she gave him from her tray on the bench.

"How long have you been here with me?" he asked after a time.

She told him.

"Jason betrayed you?"

"Yes."

He looked at her from beneath hooded lids, his eyes bloodshot, his face puffy from sleep and weeping, then looked down at his hands. Slowly he raised the left hand and flexed the fingers one by one, watching the tendons pull across his scabbed knuckles. Seemingly satisfied with that hand's mobility, he examined the right with equal deliberateness. Watching him, she wondered if his seizures had caused a diminution of his intelligence.

"Your children," he said, still playing with his fingers, "all dead?"

"Medeius may still be alive on Mt. Pelion."

Hercules didn't seem to hear, busy now flexing his toes and watching the light play across the tendons of his feet. His large toes were as thick as her wrists.

"The gods will punish Jason," he said.

"That won't change the fact that he betrayed me, murdered my children and banished me from Corinth!" To control the anger Hercules' laconic remark had roused, she got up and crossed the room to the other window. From there she could see, high in the night sky, three bright new stars. As Circe had promised in the dream.

"Tell me that story," Hercules said softly. And she did. He listened without comment and when she had finished, his face was as wet with tears as was her own. There was a lyre hanging from a peg in the wall behind his bed. He took the instrument down and began to pluck the strings, not playing, simply punctuating his thoughts in a minor key.

"The Thebans will learn that you are here, Medea,

and that you healed me. My servants will talk—if they haven't already. News of your fire will travel from Corinth. When it does—I can't keep you safe here."

"But you are Hercules."

"Yes. Hercules—who murdered his wife and sons, the daughter and grandsons of the king of Thebes." The lyre echoed his mocking tone. "Hercules, who harbors Queen Medea, who killed the king of Thebes and his daughter, my wife's younger sister—"

"A sister and a father who planned to take from me all that was mine! And without the courage of declaring war!"

"To the Thebans you will be simply a murderess," he said bluntly. "And a barbarian. Not Greek. Not Theban. Not human. To them Corinth was never yours but Jason's, and he had divorced you. No. I'll do what I can, but I can't keep you safe here."

She turned to the stars, finding solace in heaven when there was none on earth. "If I am immortal, than I have no need of safety," she said with a humorless laugh. "But mortal or immortal, I need a home—shelter." When some moments passed with no response from Hercules, she turned around to see; he had fallen back to sleep, a sad smile on his face.

Days passed. A delegation came from the Theban council bearing a petition demanding that "the witch Medea be banished from Thebes." Hercules refused to see them.

He was no longer dangerous. He had recovered physically but would not leave his room. He was ashamed of himself, ashamed to be seen by anyone. Even the servants had to call out a warning as they approached his door so that he could hide himself until they'd gone. During the day he kept the shutters closed and sat brooding in the gloom. At night he stood by the window and in a grumbling whisper begged the gods to tell him what he must do to atone for his terrible crimes.

Medea tried to reason with him, but without success.

She was standing at her window one night, looking up at her three stars and listening to him talking to the sky from his room below, when it came to her that so long as he kept on like this, he could avoid doing anything else—including breaking his promise to her.

Not so long before, such an understanding would have angered her; now it only added to her grief. For she understood also that she had been doing much the same thing—hiding here, waiting for someone else to take responsibility for her. She was stronger than Hercules, where strength counted. She would free him of his promise by leaving, by going north to Mt. Pelion to find her son—if he was still alive—and then go on to make a place for herself somewhere outside of Greece.

The decision gave her an odd sense of euphoria; she no longer expected anything of anyone and could never again be disappointed.

An old moon hung low over the mountains as she led the white mare from the stables. The cypress trees were all blackness and pine scent. By the time she rode clear of the grove, the moon had set. For all the darkness, the mare moved surely, as if she, too, was glad to be getting away.

It was that still time between night and dawn when the night hunters have gone back to their dens and the creatures of daylight still sleep, when the air chills and the birds have yet to waken. The only sound was the mare's hoofbeats, which seemed to grow lighter and faster with each passing mile.

Medea too felt lighter, almost giddy, as if she had escaped at long last from a tedious enchantment, bewitched by the promises of heroes. It was all she could do not to sing, though she hadn't sung in years. Jason had felt it was undignified for his queen to sing, and the Corinthians were afraid, or said they were, that she could cast spells with songs. The urge persisted, and when Thebes and its outlying settlements lay far behind, she decided there was no one to hear and object. She sang a hymn to dawn, to the east, and home.

When the mare pricked up her ears and whinnied, as if hearing another horse, she hushed to listen, then stopped, dismounted, and led the mare into the trees. Whoever was coming was riding hard, as if in pursuit. Had Theban sentries seen her go? Did they have hopes of killing her in revenge, out here in the wild?

The sun was almost up when a single rider galloped over the rise. It was Hercules, mounted on a huge gray stallion with hooves the size of cooking pots. In the cool air, steam rose from the horse's nostrils, and its flanks were foamy with sweat from the effort of galloping with so much weight on its back. In addition to a sack slung over one shoulder, Hercules wore his bedraggled lion's pelt and was armed with spear, sword, and shield as well as his battle club. He looked more grimly fierce than any warrior she had ever seen.

No sooner had they topped the rise than the stallion, for no apparent reason, shied and reared. Hercules slid off backward and landed on his rump. Instead of bolting, the animal came around and apologetically nuzzled the head of his rider. To Medea's relief and surprise, Hercules broke into a roar of laughter and fondled the horse's nose. "You get tired of carrying me, don't you?" he said as the horse nodded its great head up and down. "And to think I rescued you from Troy. You've no sense of gratitude."

As the horse snorted and began to crop the grass beside him, Hercules pushed himself to his feet slowly, rubbing his buttocks, then stooped to pick up his scattered weapons. Suddenly he glanced about and sniffed, then whirled to glare into the thicket where she watched. In his hunter's stance was something dangerously feral.

"Hercules?" she called, to stave off attack, and came out into the open. "Why are you following me?"

He pushed back the lion helmet and stood staring down at her. Slowly the ferocity left his face, replaced by chagrin. "Why did you leave me?"

"Why did you follow?"

He hesitated, then shrugged shyly. "Because . . . we are alike. Because I . . . we—no, I failed you," he concluded. "I'm sorry."

"We are alike," she agreed. "We're no help to one another but only add to the other's burden."

"Your knowledge cured me of my madness."

"And your sad need gave me direction when I had none."

He thought this over, then sighed and sat down on a nearby boulder, as if understanding wearied him. "I remember when I was a boy—all of life looked so easy. So glad. I was sure the years ahead would be full of nothing but glory and adventure. By my own goodness I hoped to change the world, to make mankind better for my having been born."

"And I wanted to be a queen of light and grace, bringing knowledge to my people, easing their lives with learning, giving back to Mother Earth what she gave to us," she said softly, sitting down beside him. "Oh, Hercules, look what we've done with the serpent's red egg of potential."

"Did the gods betray us by letting us become what we are?" he asked plaintively. "By making us what we are? Or did we betray them?"

"Does it matter now? Can we go back and change anything?"

"No," he admitted, "but maybe we can try again to be what those children thought they would become."

"Maybe."

Silence fell between them. In a grove nearby, a wood thrush began its morning song, and she thought of her mother and that long-ago night when she'd watched her ride away. "So-sweet," sang a bird. Challenged by the liquid notes, other birds began to sing. As if roused by the sounds, Hercules sighed, then reached out and gently covered her hand with one of his huge paws. Their eyes met.

"I am on my way to Delphi. As an immortal, I cannot bear to live forever with this guilt. It will drive me mad again. Perhaps the Pythoness can tell me what I must do to make amends, to free myself of all the ghosts that walk with me. Will you come along?"

"No. Your Pythoness can't free me of my ghosts. I must do that alone. But first I must find Medeius—if he is still alive."

"And then?"

"Go away and heal myself, as an animal does when it's wounded."

"Can you? Can that be done?"

"I don't know. Perhaps. If I can reach back to where the pain began. If I seek the Goddess's help and forgiveness."

As the sun rose, they rode north together until they came to a place where the track forked. She took the eastern road. He turned west, toward Delphi.

They never met again.

FIFTEEN

ONE MORNING SHE STOOD ON A WINDY HILL and saw the palace of Iolcus in the distance. Ten years hadn't changed this kingdom she'd won for Jason—and which he had so easily let go. The land and people still looked as poor as she remembered, as if the return of the Sacred Fleece had failed to lift some older curse.

"The curse of poverty, no doubt," she could hear her father's voice saying. To see this place brought back so many memories. How long ago it seemed since that evening at the Dawn Palace when she walked out the kitchen gate and down the hill to the stable. How far that path had led. To have no news of home in all this time . . .

She fought back the sudden ache of longing and mounted the mare. Grieving would change nothing, and it wasn't wise to linger here. Not because anyone would recognize her, but because they were so poor and would see only a lone woman riding a valuable mare and might attempt to kill her for the horse.

On the plains between Mt. Pelion and the sea, great herds of horses grazed, watched over by the tribes of King Chiron the centaur, whose palace was a vast cave within the mountainside. Unlike other centaurs, who had a reputation for wild and lascivious behavior, Chiron was renowned as a sage and prophet. He was learned in medicine, philosophy, and war. Half the kings of Greece sent him their sons to be schooled. So Jason had told her, but then Jason often lied.

Medea had never seen a centaur and suspected them to be creatures of Greek fancy and ignorance, like so many of the monsters they feared and revered. Since his people worshipped horses, she assumed Chiron was a priest–king who, for ceremonial occasions, dressed in the hide of a stallion to awe his people. His name would be a title passed from father to son.

On the worn track leading to Chiron's mountain, the mare began to skitter and dance at every blowing leaf until Medea was hard put to keep her from bolting. Leaning forward to pat the horse's neck, she saw an old man watching from the bushes on the slope ahead. His eyes were bright and kindly. He had long white hair, a curly gray beard, and was remarkably well muscled for his age. He appeared to be naked from the waist up.

It wasn't until he moved toward her that she realized what he was by the peculiar rocking motion of his upper body. Instinctively, like her mare, she wanted to bolt from this monstrosity, this black and silver stallion's body with a virile old man growing out of its chest.

As he walked, he swished flies with his tail and his hooves left neat patterns in the dusty track. He stopped so close to her nervous mare that she could smell his horsey odor. Still without speaking, he bent his forelegs, knelt on all four knees and, using his hands to brace himself, lowered himself until he was facedown in the dust.

"No! Stop!" she cried, disturbed to receive obeisance, especially from this creature. "Rise! Why should you prostrate yourself before me?"

He got up awkwardly, leaving hand prints amid the hoofprints on the track, and brushed off the dust. When he spoke, his voice was shockingly cultured, his manner calm and self-assured. "I greet you with the respect you deserve, Queen Medea. I am only Chiron the centaur. What you are is far older, far more powerful. You represent life and death. I am only an ideal perverted. You will live as long as man. My entire race is dying."

"Even if you know me, you can't know what I've done. What I—"

"I was expecting you." His lined face filled with sadness as he backed away and turned, beckoning her to follow. "I saw visions in the flames, pictures of you and your fire at Corinth, and of your poor children. I cannot judge what you are guilty of—I leave that to the gods—who themselves are not without fault. I have done what I could. I have kept your eldest—and now *only*—son safe and well."

"Ah!" Her relief exploded in a cry of gladness. "I was so afraid. So—"

He waved a brawny arm in dismissal of any expression of gratitude. "The boy was given to me to protect and teach—just as his father once was."

"Did his father come here this winter?"

"He came." With a whicker of wings, a flock of doves flew up from their dust bath in the track ahead. Chiron stopped and folded his arms across his chest, watching the birds until they lit on a distant ledge. "This boy whom I raised from helpless infancy, this prince whom I saved from sure death, this man who you made king, came here—smelling of hate and fear, wanting to murder his own son."

The old horse king swished his tail in anger. "To violate my teaching so! To foul my esteem for him! To spoil fond memories! I took his weapons from him and sent him away. He's unfit to be called noble!"

She urged her reluctant mare ahead to walk beside the old centaur, and they traveled in silence for a time.

"Yesterday a message came from Thebes." Chiron broke the silence. "Jason claims your sorcery made him marry you, that he could divorce you only after breaking the spell you had cast over him. He says that you gave him Corinth and on the day of his marriage to the Theban, you set fire to the palace. When the flames spread, he claims that you fled to the roof where, in a witch's rage of murder and revenge, you stabbed his children to death. After which, you called down from the sky a chariot drawn by dragons—winged, fire-breathing snakes—and flew away in it."

"Who would believe all that?"

"Many. Because they want to," he said, and she knew that was true.

The road passed through barley fields, orchards, and vineyards on the mountain's slope. Men and centaurs worked in the fields, women in the vineyards, pruning the vines so that each grape cluster would receive a full share of sunlight. Above the orchards on the north side of the palace gateway was a practice field, where centaurs and young warriors were training. To the right was archery practice, on the left spears flew, and in between sword and club combat was being taught. From the distance the noise suggested woodsmen and smithies gone berserk.

As she and Chiron drew closer, she caught sight of Medeius. The boy was hurling spears at a stuffed boar hide. Poised to throw, he hesitated and turned to look down the path. Suddenly he dropped his spear and ran to meet her. The centaur who was his trainer yelled after him and, when Medeius did not stop, galloped in pursuit. He would have run him down had Chiron not intervened.

She gave silent thanks to the Goddess as she embraced her son, her beautiful child, the only person left on earth for her to love, and she cried as she held him close.

"My father was here," Medeius said when they were alone together. "If I hadn't been out hunting with Icadius . . ." He searched her face. "Is it true? Did you burn . . . uh . . . Did he banish you? Did he kill my brothers and sister?"

"It's all true."

His eyes filled with tears, which he did his best to blink away. "He said once, when we were small, Argus and I, that we'd be lucky to reach manhood alive. We'd been playing under his window. Argus thought he was just angry because we'd wakened him, but I believed then that he meant it. He never wanted us to have Corinth."

"The gods will deal with him," she said, hoping that was true. "He's betrayed them, too."

"Where will we go, Mother?"

"You will stay here, with Chiron. He'll protect you. I must find a place for myself."

"Can't you stay here, too?"

"No. I must leave at dawn. I have too many enemies. If I stayed, you and Chiron's people might suffer for my presence."

"But where will you go, Mother?"

"Where there are no other people."

"Will I ever see you again? Or am I to lose you, too?"

"We'll be together again—when it is safe."

"You swear?"

"I swear!"

Chiron's palace smelled like a well-kept stable, redolent with sweet hay. The centaurs and their slaves were gracious and showed her every respect. In her guest chamber late that night, she heard murmurings from deep within the labyrinth of corridors and tunnels in the cave, sounds that made her recall the cave and Temple of the Goddess. And in her dreams, she remembered all that she had been, and all that she had done, and saw too clearly what she had become, what she had done with her knowledge.

In the morning she traded the crown she had worn as Corinth's queen and bought slaves and goods from Chiron. With them she traveled north along the coast until she had passed beyond the borders of all known kingdoms.

In a deserted land she built a small villa in the Colchian style, a rectangle around an inner court, with a square tower beside the gate. The house stood against a hill and commanded a sweeping view of the sea. When the building was complete, the fields cleared and crops and vineyard planted, Chiron came to visit. When he left, he took more than half of the slaves back with him. She wanted no more people around her than was absolutely necessary.

She lived alone in exile and, other than Chiron, had few visitors. Because she was still numb with grief and shock, whole seasons passed without her noticing. She busied herself with manual labor and went to bed exhausted so that she might get at least a few hours of sleep. Then a spring came that she saw was beautiful, and she felt her interest in life reawakening. When Chiron came again, she rode back with him to visit her son. Medeius had grown taller and even more handsome, and she felt great pride.

She resumed her studies, sometimes frightening her servants. They would see unnatural light flickering in the windows of her tower room and claim they saw spirits, shapechangers, fearsome creatures from the darkness of their own imaginations. And she let them think that; awe kept them obedient.

She would disappear for days, riding alone into the mountains, sometimes traveling in disguise. Once she went as far as Egypt, but usually she went only to Mt. Pelion to take Medeius gifts and reassurance. The servants could have run away in her absences, but they didn't; for all they feared her, they had never lived so well.

Five years passed quickly. And while she was alone, she was never quite so lonely as she had been in Greece. No one here called her barbarian. With thought and prayer, the time came when she could remember her dead children without weeping, and Jason without rage. But she forgot nothing. And hoped for nothing.

One morning she walked out of the sea after her daily bath to find Circe waiting, seated on a driftwood log. Circe wore a shepherd's cloak, perhaps to keep the slaves from talking, should they see her. Beautiful women did not appear out of nowhere in this isolated area, while cloaked shepherds sometimes seemed to do just that.

"Are you afraid of me now?" said Circe, seeing her shiver.

"No. Once I was. Now I'm simply cold."

Circe raised a hand and stopped the wind. She pointed a finger at Medea's robe, and the garment obligingly flew up and wrapped itself around its naked owner.

"Does your presence here mean you've forgiven me?" Medea asked, calmly belting her robe.

"There's no question of forgiveness. Your actions never harmed me."

"You never punished me for going against your teachings."

A rueful smile lit Circe's face. "I didn't have to; you did that yourself when you married Jason. Now forget about yourself and listen. I came here for a purpose. Aeetes has lost his throne. He spent all his time brooding about the past and ignored the present. His brother Perses saw his chance and took Colchis from him."

"He's dead?" Medea asked, alarmed. In her mind time stood still in Colchis. All there remained as it had been when she went away, with nothing changed except her absence from the scene. She couldn't imagine the Dawn Palace without Aeetes.

"He's not dead," said Circe. "He's in hiding."

"That must please you—to see an old enemy defeated."

"That I feel my brother's misery is deserved is unimportant," Circe said. "What matters is that Colchis is your land—your mother's land. Do you want Perses to keep it? He will—if you remain here and do nothing. But if you stay here, then my teaching and time were truly wasted, and you will do nothing that matters with your knowledge. I've said what I came to say. You do what you will."

Circe stood, and a breeze ruffled Medea's hair. With a swirl of her cloak, Circe turned, the cloak became wings and just that quickly she was gone. In her place a falcon stood on the driftwood log. It deliberately adjusted its wing feathers and fixed Medea with a ruthless golden eye, blinked and took flight.

As she watched the falcon soar, she thought of that long-ago day when Jason came striding up the hill to the Dawn Palace. Among the men following him had been her uncle Perses. She could only vaguely remember what he looked like now. And he had taken Colchis.

Her eyes stung from staring at the sky, and when the falcon disappeared, she rested her gaze on the soft blue clouds piled above the sea. Beyond the far horizon lay her mother's land—and her mother had chosen Aeetes. She would take their grandson Medeius and go home and regain her land.

"Of all the spells I've ever cast, of all the knowledge

I've ever gained, let only the best serve me now," she prayed. And then she set to work.

Her smith was sent to his forge to make armor and arrowpoints for Medeius. Carrier pigeons were set free, messengers sent out. Within days Chiron came and brought her son with him. Medeius was a man now, strong and handsome, one year older than she had been when she ran away with Jason.

She gave her slaves their freedom, but they refused to leave, suddenly viewing this furthermost house of exile as a sanctuary instead. "Well, then," she told them, "you keep this house safe against my return; keep the fields and flocks and grapes as healthy as if they were your own. For my sake." And this they could accept.

They were watching from the hill the morning she walked down to the sea for the last time. During the night a great ship had mysteriously appeared and anchored in the shallows. On its blue sail was a white full moon. A strange crew loaded aboard the heavy crates she'd had her slaves carry to the beach.

She said good-bye to Chiron. Her thanks to him for his care of her son and for his dear friendship were as heartfelt as the tearful farewell between the old horse king and the boy. Medeius promised the day would come when he would bring his sons to be taught on Mt. Pelion. Chiron smiled and agreed, but he looked to her and both understood that he might be gone by then, his cave palace empty.

After days at sea, the morning came when she woke to see the sun rising over the snow peaks of the high Caucasus and she wept, having long ago given up hope of ever seeing this land again. With the wind bellying the sail, the ship drove straight into the broad river's currents. Entreating the aid of the Goddess in her venture, Medea stood in the wind and salt spray with her son beside her.

It had been foretold that she would return to end the rule of the usurper, Perses. From all over the countryside men who supported the old Colchian matriarchy flocked to the riverbanks to wait, and when the great ship with the moon sail appeared, they followed it upstream. Before she set foot on Colchian soil again, an army waited for her son to lead it. Ahead of that army the followers of Perses fled.

When her ship reached Aea, smoke was rising from the embers of houses torched by the fleeing forces. The marketplace was bare of stalls, the remaining houses shuttered. The palace storerooms and granaries were broken open; the barracks burned, the stables empty. On the hillsides, many of the fine old trees had been wantonly cut down. But in the distance, on its hill, the Dawn Palace stood intact, as beautiful as she remembered it to be.

The ship eased against the quay, and Medea disembarked. With her son beside her, she walked slowly up the Royal Road. Everywhere she looked there were ghosts of the past. They followed her up the palace steps and crowded through the King's Gate. More were in the deserted courtyard and with them came smells, sounds, voices—all of which she thought she had lost or forgotten. Just as she was about to enter the Hall, an absurdly fat person hustled out to greet her.

At the sight of Toas she stopped, unsure if he was real until he clasped his pudgy hands together and attempted to kneel before her, saying: "Don't enter the

Hall, Princess Medea. His men have fled, but he refuses to go. He is waiting to kill you."

"Perses?" she said and Toas nodded, his gaze respectfully on the pavement. "And how is it you are still here, Toas? Did you also betray your king?"

"Never!" His eyes met hers, protocol forgotten in his anger that she could think him capable of such disloyalty. "Nor did I cause him grief as—" At that he remembered his position and averted his gaze again. "I chose to stay alive by serving. I was given that choice or death. But it is because of me that mighty Aeetes escaped and has been well cared for. You can believe me or not, as you choose."

"I believe you," she said, touched by his bravery. "I have come to return to Aeetes the throne my mother gave to him, loyal Toas. I have brought my son, Prince Medeius." She looked around to introduce Medeius to the old chamberlain, but the young man was nowhere to be seen.

"So the Nine predicted," Toas said, referring to the priestesses. "The king will be greatly pleased."

"The queen, is she in hiding, too? And Chalciope?"

"The queen is dead, most noble one." Toas sighed, remembering. "Of a fever some three winters ago. Your noble sister is with your father."

"Where did my son go when he left my side?"

As Toas pointed to the Hall, they heard a muffled shout from inside and a faint clatter of metal against stone. Medea paled. "Call the guards!" she ordered and ran toward the open doors.

"There are no guards at the moment, most noble one," said Toas, but she didn't hear him.

After the brightness of the sun outside, the great hall was dim and smelled of wet ashes. There were paths through the litter on the floor, and the walls looked leprous with patches of fallen plaster. As her eyes adjusted to the gloom, she saw Medeius, bow in hand, standing over a robed figure slumped in Aeetes' great chair.

Hearing footsteps, her son turned, ready to draw his bow, then, seeing her, called: "Is this Perses?"

She looked and nodded. Age had made him thinner; death erased the envy that had always creased his face.

"He thought that I was you, Mother. He called your name as the arrow found its mark." As Medeius moved, his foot kicked something concealed by the fold of Perses' robe. Hearing the familiar ringing sound, Medea reached down and pulled out Aeetes' gold crown. It shivered in her hands.

She didn't go with Toas to the mountain cave where Aeetes was hidden. Instead, she sent the crown, his finest robes, and his seal ring. A golden chair was sent to carry him down the narrow trails and a chariot to meet him on the road. Chalciope and others among the court in exile, being younger, had returned some days earlier. The two sisters' pleasure at being reunited was made bittersweet by memories of all that had happened in the years apart.

Two weeks had passed since Perses' death. Of the usurper's head, piked and mounted by the marsh road, only the skull remained, the arrow shaft serving as a perch for crows. The fighting was over; spring plowing had begun. Medeius waited only for his grandfather's return before leading the army across the river to secure and regain those lands.

She watched from the palace rooftop as the royal procession wound through the city and up the Royal Road, saw it stop as Aeetes took note of some particular desecration of his property or, more frequently, acknowledged the cheers of the crowd lining the way. As the commanding general of the victorious army, Medeius waited to greet the king on the steps of the palace and to formally pledge his loyalty to the crown.

Because there was no vantage point from which she could watch discreetly, she missed her father's reaction to his first sight of this grandson, although Toas told her about it later. Aeetes, he said, had eyes for no one else once he saw the boy, and in his eagerness to welcome him, ignored Chalciope, who helped him from the chariot. Aeetes had embraced Medea's son, saying, "Here is the best of us, come home at last!" Medea had heard the cheering that greeted this acceptance.

The first thing Aeetes called for on entering the palace was a bath and barber, preferring the luxury of hot water and privacy to the feast prepared in his honor.

Afterwards she met him in the tiny courtyard of her mother's old apartment, the meeting place chosen by him—perhaps as neutral ground. He was seated on the bench beneath the grape arbor when she entered, and he appeared to be dozing. What she could not see from the rooftop was evident now. He had aged and was no longer "round as the sun"; his robes hung slack, and all his rings were loose on his fingers. He held his crown possessively against his belly, where the piece shivered and chimed with each breath, like some glorious tambour. Seeing him, she realized with great sadness that, regardless of his claim, he was not immortal.

As if wakened by her gaze, he suddenly sat erect and looked up at her, startled. "For an instant I thought you were your mother," he said after an awkward moment. After setting aside the crown, he patted the bench in invitation.

"I grieved for you," he said when she had settled down beside him. She took his hand in her own and held it. "I grieved for the others, too," he said, "but not as I grieved for you. Even your betrayal, hard as that was to accept, faded in comparison to the emptiness your absence caused. As if I were an actor and you my audience. With you gone, there was no point in performing."

"And yet you would have killed your audience the night I ran away," she reminded him.

"Oh, yes! And for years afterward," he admitted. "Of course, if I had done that, I also might have ended my days up there in that inglorious cave . . . because you wouldn't have returned. . . ." He fell silent to collect his thoughts. "I've thought since then: I was a fool. I should have given Jason the Sacred Fleece. If I had, you'd never have gone with him—he would have refused to marry you." Aeetes fell silent, remembering, and she respected his silence. "Does anything remain of my Corinth?" he asked then.

"What truly matters. The land. And Medeius."

"Medeius. Yes." Aeetes considered this. "Was *he* the point of this whole story, the reason why I came here from Corinth, why Apsyrtus died, why you fled with Jason? Is he what the gods had in mind? Or is life all uncaring circumstance—mere accident?"

She thought of Circe's tapestry, the altered patterns, the discarded threads. "There is a pattern, a purpose, but we can't see it clearly."

"And do the gods direct it, do you think?"

She shook her head, not sure if his gods were part of her beliefs. "I believe the Goddess does, and we are aspects of her power."

"And does that faith comfort you?"

"Sometimes," she said.

At nightfall she walked up to the temple. Since returning, she had spent most of each evening here. The serenity of the place was soothing. In all the chaos of the past months, few of the priestesses had had the time or opportunity to attend to temple duties; they counted themselves lucky to have a servant keep a few lamps lit and the place free of wildlife. Even so, a number of large bats now hung from the ceiling, and two pursued the moths attracted by the lamplight.

In the flickering gloom she seated herself on the lowest step of the pedestal and let the tension of the day drain into the cool silence around her. A moth hissed like an ember as it died in a flame. A bat squeaked, and she heard the sound echo off the ceiling. From the corridors and passages came a faint roar that failed to completely mask the whispers of the old creatures down below.

She looked up at the statue; the Goddess did not change. She was a surety, serene and everlasting in the uncertainty of life. She would be for each generation what they needed her to be—which would in no way alter what she truly was.

The same rule applied to herself, Medea thought,

and to Circe, and to her mother. In a century or two, no one would remember what they were now, or had been; and if they were thought of at all, it would be in the spirit of that future time. Which was as it should be.

AUTHOR'S NOTES

When Jason and Medea met, perhaps in 1300 B.C.:
Linen, cotton, and silk were all used in clothing.
Chickens had been domesticated for at least a thousand years.
The comet we call Halley's had been named and watched for by astronomers in Egypt, Babylonia, India, and China.
There were cities with vast libraries with tablets in eight languages.
There were palaces with heated floors, flush toilets, bathtubs, and charcoal-filtered drinking water.
Troy had been sacked or destroyed by earthquakes at least six times and was about to be destroyed and rebuilt for the seventh.

In short, the world was not as young and primitive as the Greek myths would lead one to believe. In fairness, it must be noted that the origins of many of the myths are far older than the Greeks, some dating back beyond written history. Each story exists in several, often contradictory, versions from overlapping cultures and religions.

To illustrate the confusion: Jason's mother is known by eight different names. The same adventures are attributed to Jason, Hercules, Ulysses, Theseus, and others, the same wicked acts to Medea, Medusa, and Circe.

Considering not only the myths but the character assessment in the Medea operas and Euripides' tragedy of the same name, I was interested to read in Robert Graves' scholarly work *The Greek Myths* that Euripides (484–406 B.C.) was paid fifteen talents of silver by the citizens of Corinth to write a play absolving *them* of any guilt in the murders of Medea's children. Graves quotes Hyginus's *Fabula* (a collection of essays on myths, circa 10 B.C.); Servius, a late fourth-century A.D. Roman grammarian and scholar, and Scholiast's study of Euripides' *Medea*.

The reason for the Corinthians' commissioning the play was that, according to a story current in the Golden Age, the citizens of Corinth had taken revenge on Medea by stoning all her children to death in the Temple of Hera, where her children had taken refuge, and then burning the bodies as an offering to the Goddess. Corinth was once a religious center for a god who required infants to be sacrificed as burnt offerings to appease his wrath, a barbaric reputation the Corinthians wanted to live down.

They received their money's worth. Euripides' play not only won that year's drama prize, but his propaganda-as-art became the accepted version of Medea's story.

Medea, a foreigner, high priestess of a female god, heiress to Corinth, daughter of a mighty king, skilled as a healer and herbalist, would not have represented the Greek ideal of a properly ignorant and submissive female—even before she burned her palace.

It should perhaps be noted here that the much-vaunted Golden Age of Greece, when many of these myths became popular folklore, was golden only for those citizens lucky enough to have been born male, free, and landowning. In that Golden Age there were five slaves for every free man. Unwanted infants were exposed on a hill to die. Women, even those from the wealthiest families, were little more than chattels.

Pythagoras (582–506 B.C.) had defined the universe as being created by the tension between moral opposites—the Good principle, which created order, light, and man, and the Evil principle, which created chaos, darkness and—you guessed it—woman. This misogynist doctrine permeates Greek myth.

Some writers claim Medea and Jason were in their mid- to late twenties when they met, with Medea being older and Jason an innocent youth. Others say both were younger. Since both were still unmarried in an age when to be fourteen was to be a mature adult and parent, and thirty was *old*, it seemed logical to me that they were in their teens.

All accounts agree that Jason and Medea's marriage lasted ten years but disagree widely on the number of their children. The count ranges from four to fourteen—seven boys and seven girls. Fairly consistent is the fact that their eldest son was Medeius and one daughter was named Eriopus.

According to Euripides, and the writers who used him as a reference, Medea's jealous rage was so great that she stabbed two of Jason's sons to death on the palace rooftop before fleeing in the chariot pulled by winged, fire-breathing dragons—while the rest of her children were burning to death in the palace. The murders are thus the deliberate act of a savage seeking revenge on her betrayer. Yet all the ancient myths describe Medea as a learned herbalist and healer. She is credited with saving the lives of several Argonauts during the return voyage. In none of the pre-Euripides stories is she said to have killed her children.

Logically, and legally, if she wished to retain Corinth as her inheritance, she would have had a far better chance of doing so with Jason's sons. Add to this the fact that she *was* a healer, and it seems even less likely that she would kill her children.

On the other hand, since Jason intended to usurp the throne of Corinth, to do so he would have had to dispose of all of Medea's children—the legitimate heirs. Otherwise they would have disposed of their father as soon as possible.

There is also the point that if Medea had wanted to kill her children out of sheer hatred for their father, she wouldn't have waited until the last minute before fleeing a burning palace. While she was obsessed with Jason, in none of the myths is she ever depicted as stupid.

Some myths say Medeius was also killed at Corinth and that Medea later married an Asian king and had another son by him, whom she also named Medeius. It is also said that after leaving Hercules and Thebes, she went to Athens and wed King Aegeus, but was banished for attempting to poison his son Theseus so that her son might inherit the Athenian throne; that she went to Italy and became a snake charmer; that she had other evil adventures before returning to Colchis with Medeius to restore Aeetes to his throne; that Zeus fell in love with her because he admired her spunk and so made her immortal.

After years of homeless wandering, Jason returned at last to the place where the *Argo* had been beached. Sitting in the ship's shade and grieving for the wealth and glory he had lost, he decided to hang himself from the prow. Before he could get up to find a rope, the old boat suddenly lurched forward and crushed him to death.

I found that satisfying.

While there are many different versions of the *Argo*'s return route, most accounts agree that she sailed around the northern shore of the Black Sea. Some say the Colchian ships caught up with the *Argo* near the mouth of the Danube—where Medea supposedly killed Apsyrtus with a sword and flung his body into the sea. Others say that Jason killed both Aeetes and Apsyrtus before leaving the Dawn Palace. One story has Atalanta spearing Aeetes with her lance and him dying of the wound. Another says that when the Colchians trapped the *Argo*, Medea was put ashore on an island and devised a plot to lure Apsyrtus there so that Jason might kill him. That the boy was quickly hacked to pieces suggests to me that a strong warrior was his killer.

After Apsyrtus's death, geography makes it impossible to reconcile many of the myths associated with the *Argo*'s return journey. Some say the ship returned to the Phasis River, repassing the city of Aea, and came out in the Caspian Sea. The Phasis (now called the Rioni) does not connect the two seas. Some say the *Argo* sailed up the Danube and Save rivers and down the Po and out into the Adriatic and there came to Circe's island. Also impossible. Another story claims they sailed up the Don and out into the Gulf of Finland, thus visiting the cold northern land of Hyperborea, and came home past England, Spain, and Italy. This version explains why one myth has the *Argo* landing at Corfu when "first reaching Greek waters," where Jason and Medea are at last married.

I have chosen the most probable return route, thus skipping the tale of a storm that blew the *Argo* into the middle of the desert in Libya, forcing the crew to put the ship on rollers and push it across the sands to a lake, which led to a river, and from there to the coast and Crete. Also ignored is a trip to Armenia and a stop at Elba.

The earliest known intact statues of the Great Mother Goddess date back to 25,000 B.C. Some as old as 30,000 B.C. have been found in caves, smashed beyond repair. In style they range from the grossly erotic to almost prim; in mood from benign to bloody. Worship of her was the prime religion for over 25,000 years.

In antiquity the term *barbarian* was used to describe either an uncivilized person or a foreigner. It was quite often a pejorative term.

There is no general agreement as to where Circe's island was. I have, for the sake of geography, located it among the islands at the mouth of the Danube. Since Circe, like Medea and her mother Asterodeia, is an aspect of the Great Goddess, only she knows where her island truly is.

At the time of this story, Greece did not exist as a country. The name is used here as a generic to avoid the confusion of too many ancient and unfamiliar names.

Modern-day archaeology has revealed that Colchis was the ancient name for what is now part of the People's Republic of Georgia, USSR, although no one is sure of the ancient borders, nor has the capital city, Aea, been found to date. Before written history and after, tribe after tribe from beyond the Caspian Sea had passed through this area en route to the Black Sea, the Balkans, Greece and northern Europe. They brought with them their various goddesses, gods, and totems—including bull and ram cults. Shrines to both have been found, along with proof that both the Egyptians and the Hittites used Colchis as a colony, a source of gold, silver, obsidian, and slaves. Fleeces are still placed in the streams in Georgia to trap floating gold dust.

SOME OF THE REFERENCE SOURCES

Alsop, Joseph. *From the Silent Earth.* New York: Harper & Row, 1964.

Bulfinch's Mythology. New York: The Nelson Doubleday Co., 1968.

Dothan, Trude. "Lost Outpost of the Egyptian Empire." *National Geographic* 162 (December 1982) pp. 739–768.

Gore, Rick. "The Mediterranean." *National Geographic* 162 (December 1982) pp. 694–736.

Graves, Robert. *The Greek Myths.* 2 vols. New York: Penguin Books, 1960.

Grun, Bernard. *The Timetables of History, a Horizontal Linkage of People and Events.* New York: Touchstone Books, 1963.

Justin, Dena. "From Mother Goddess to Dishwasher." *Smithsonian* (April 1977) pp. 41–44.

Renfrew, Colin, ScD. "Ancient Europe Is Older Than We Thought." *National Geographic* 152 (November 1977) pp. 615–626.